The Best Actors That Ever Lived

GARY LEE VINCENT

Burning Bulb
PUBLISHING

The Best Actors That Ever Lived
By **Gary Lee Vincent**

Burning Bulb Publishing
P.O. Box 4721
Bridgeport, WV 26330-4721
United States of America
www.BurningBulbPublishing.com

Cover by James Aaron Hislope.

First Edition.

Paperback Edition ISBN: 978-1-948278-37-9

Printed in the United States of America

Dedicated to Greg Mason,
who inspires me to always be my best.

CHAPTER 1

The old Barnaby Theater sat on the corner of the city of Tucson's Broadway and Brookwood streets. It was one of the kinds of buildings that people said had 'character,' this meaning that though it was old and dilapidated and in danger of being marked for demolition by the town authorities, the Barnaby Theater created a feeling of nostalgia in those who knew its long history. Most of the folk who'd grown up in the neighborhood, meaning the old-timers, would walk by the Barnaby wistfully recalling the good old days before videotape rentals (and now Netflix and digital streaming), when their parents went to watch plays there.

The building was moderately sized. It had three floors with an amphitheater that had a wraparound gallery on the second floor.

Bob Barnaby stood staring down into the street from the window of his third-floor office in the Barnaby Theater. It was early June and, this morning, the end-of-spring weather was just fine.

For a while Bob watched the vehicles and people that were crossing the intersection.

Bob Barnaby was thirty-four years old, had dark eyes and hair and was a bit overweight. The latest in the long line of Barnaby proprietors of the eponymously named family establishment/ property/heirloom, the young man currently wished he'd followed his long-dead mother's advice and gone into stock trading instead.

But no, dad insisted that I work in the theater and take over from him and now look at me!

As if his thoughts were an instruction to himself, Bob did step back from the window and look at his reflection in the large mirror hung on the wall to the left of his desk.

Bob always took great care with his personal appearance. But, staring at himself now, six foot two in his socks and wearing a really faded blue shirt, equally faded dark pants, and extremely scuffed brown shoes...there was no hiding the fact that he was broke and that his clothes had all been washed one time too many.

He sighed and wished the phone would ring and give him some good news.

He checked his watch and then walked over to sit on the edge of his desk.

Lisa should've called me by now.

Lisa Manning was Bob's lawyer. She handled all of Bob and the theater's legal matters and kept Bob out of contractual and financial difficulties. Or at least, she tried to. At the moment, things weren't really working out for the Barnaby Theater and Troupe. Bob hadn't been able to pay anyone's wages for two months and now lived in perpetual dread of the actors quitting on him.

It wasn't really Bob's fault. Bob had inherited the Barnaby Troupe along with the theater, and in deference to his late father's memory had tried to make a go of it.

Although Bob had a bachelor's degree in Theatre Arts, he neither acted himself nor directed the thespians he employed. That task was handled by Case and Helen Miller, a married pair who'd been with the troupe since his father's days. The Millers were very experienced actors, and Bob had quickly realized that he'd do best to let them do what they did best and concentrate his own energies on promotion and running the operation.

And, following this approach, they'd at first had quite a bit of success. The troupe—fifteen persons in all—had put on several very well-received dramas; their *Death of a Salesman* had been praised by all the critics, and after a while word had spread that Bob Barnaby was keeping alive the old theater traditions begun by his grandfathers in the post-colonial days. The Barnaby became the place to go to see well-acted plays...though to help finances along, Bob did allow the occasional rock band to perform here, something the troupe disliked.

At first there had been a rise. Not a meteoric one, but enough success that Bob could comfortably pay everyone, pay the theater's utilities, and still have enough money left over to feel that he was doing relatively well in life.

But then . . .

But then had come *Airplane Story*. *Airplane Story* was a play by Wilson Reeves. This witty tale of the onboard and off-board trials of a flight crew had seemed great on paper, and even during rehearsals. But it had tanked. The Barnaby Troupe's performance of *Airplane Story* had tanked catastrophically, said 'catastrophe' being largely due to the fact that *Airplane Story* had required an elaborate set (which had included an expensive full-scale facsimile of an airplane's interior) which had both emptied Bob's bank account, and which also, against his lawyer Lisa's repeated warnings, had seen him mortgage the theater building (which belonged to his family) to raise the money.

The *Airplane Story* disaster had been the beginning of the end. Seemingly like dark magic or the results of a curse, all of the theater critics' goodwill vanished overnight. The play's reviews were so universally bad that the Barnaby Theater became a pariah location, with no one wishing to be associated with a place that produces "Garbage that even a trio of deaf, dumb and blind monkeys would be unwilling to sit through," as one critic put it; while another proclaimed, "We thought that young Bob Barnaby had it in him—that spark of genius that his father and grandfather possessed—that understanding of what constitutes good drama; well, folks, we were damn wrong, weren't we?" And as a female socialite had cattily commented while under the influence of copious amounts of alcohol, "*Airplane Story?* Oh, that was such a wonderful piece of trash. Bob Barnaby should be ashamed of himself—he's nowhere near half the director that his father was. But it won't be hard for Bob to make amends for *Airplane Story*. All he has to do is stick a gun in his mouth and blow his brains out. That'll be much more dramatic that his stupid play was."

This lady critic had no idea how close she was to the actual state of affairs. Because, many were the dark nights then when Bob did consider putting a gun in his mouth and blowing himself away. That he hadn't killed himself was entirely due to the support of his loving girlfriend Jane Piper. After *Airplane Story* crashed and burned, Jane had sat beside Bob night after night, patching up his tattered ego and filling him with hope again.

"Everything's gonna be alright, baby," she'd kept telling him. "Just you wait and see. Sure, it looks really bad, but it ain't the end of the world." She'd smile nicely. "Yes, I know that at the moment you don't like to hear mention of anything to do with the sky, but, baby, you'll soon discover that every cloud really does have a silver lining."

***

Thinking of Jane Piper, a thin smile came to Bob's lips. Oh, Jane was everything to him. She was the sun that shone in his sky, the light that lit up his life. Bob had no idea what he'd do without Jane.

Then a bitter taste filled his mouth and his smile became a frown. He and Jane should have been married by now. They'd been scheduled to tie the knot after the premiere of *Airplane Story*. But once the play tanked, so had their marital plans.

Of course, they could have simply gone before a Justice of the Peace and done it quietly, but no...Jane wanted a big wedding and at that point they couldn't afford one; after the *Airplane Story* debacle Bob could barely afford to buy gas into his old pickup truck, and he'd considered going on a diet of cat food.

Then the smile returned to Bob's face. *But, hey, it ain't over yet. Soon...very soon...I'll have some money again and Jane can have her lavish wedding. I just hope nothing goes wrong this time.*

Then he frowned again. *Oh, but why hasn't Lisa called me yet? Will the bank advance me the funds I need to pay everyone and prevent them rioting?*

Due to the mortgage that Bob had taken out to finance *Airplane Story*, his bank now essentially owned the Barnaby Theater. A clause in the mortgage contract gave Bob a twelve-month option to repurchase the building, but there were just two months left of that grace period, and Bob had no way to repay the loan he'd taken. Rather than giving the bank any money, he was trying to get an additional loan from them.

Bob grimaced at the depths to which he'd sunk. Oh, these were indeed bad times.

The bank manager wasn't talking to Bob anymore; but Lisa and the manager were family friends, so she was interceding on Bob's behalf.

Bob couldn't help but think something had gone wrong with Lisa's meeting with the bank manager. He restrained the urge to call her and instead walked over to stare out of the window again.

***

At the moment, the Barnaby Drama Troupe were rehearsing *Marriage and Divorce*, a play that Jane had found somewhere on the internet by Rich Bottles, a barely known writer. *Marriage and Divorce* was a great play, one detailing the ups and downs of several couple's love lives. It was a bittersweet comedy and the Barnaby Troupe's actors and actresses all loved it.

Even Bob's lawyer Lisa Manning loved it.

Bob was certain the play would be a hit and would put the Barnaby Theater back on the theater map. But despite this, he was doing his best not to be optimistic. Bob didn't even dare be 'cautiously optimistic.' Bob of course knew that in situations such as this optimism was greatly to be desired, but he felt he had full justification to be worried:

I felt equally optimistic about Airplane Story, and look what happened then!

Unable to remain still while waiting for his phone to ring with either good or bad news, Bob left the window and crossed to the door of his office. He opened the door and listened. If he strained his ears from up here he could catch the sounds of the troupe rehearsing.

He listened for a while but heard nothing. He was unsure if the silence was a good omen or a bad one.

Bob stuck his head out and peered cautiously along the corridor. The passageway was empty save for Dave Ferguson the janitor, who was busy mopping. The old man, dressed in a blue one-piece work outfit and also sporting a faded denim hat, turned around and caught Bob's eye.

'Fergie' leaned on his mop and waved. "Morning, boss," he greeted, a smile creasing his already age-creased face. "Nice day today."

Bob waved back and tried to smile. "Morning, Fergie." Bob had inherited Dave Ferguson along with the theater; and if Bob's father was to be believed, he'd also inherited Fergie from Bob's grandfather. The grey-haired old man was a good sort, kindly and helpful, and everyone liked him.

Before Fergie could resume mopping, Bob asked, "Hey, do you know why everywhere is so quiet? I thought the guys were rehearsing. I know I saw Case and Helen arriving in their pickup a short while ago."

Fergie shrugged. "They *were* rehearsing earlier, but now they're having a meeting of some sort; that's why it's quiet downstairs. I dunno what the meeting's about though."

On hearing the word 'meeting,' a shiver of fear went through Bob. But then he shrugged it off. "Thanks, Fergie," he waved at the old man.

Fergie resumed his mopping and Bob retreated back into his office.

What are they meeting about? he worried. *It can't be about their unpaid wages. I've already assured everyone that they'll get their money today once the bank . . .*

His cellphone rang then. Bob gave a start as it jerked him out of his thoughts, then heaved a sigh of relief when he saw that Lisa was the caller. Finally!

He accepted the call. "Hi, girl. How'd it go with Brody?" Liam Brody was almost the same age as Dave Ferguson, the Barnaby's janitor, and a very strict sort of fellow. He and Bob's father had been high school classmates. Lisa, who was forty-seven years old, knew the Brodys well; she'd been a bridesmaid at Brody's daughter's wedding.

Lisa's voice was flat. "I'm sorry, Bob, but he didn't change his stance. 'No loan for Bob Barnaby under any circumstances,' is what he told me."

"But didn't you offer him—I mean the bank— part of the show's profits as collateral like we agreed?"

Lisa sighed. Her voice over the line sounded like she was carrying a weight on her shoulders. "I did, Bobby, of course I did. He flatly refused to bite the bait." She sighed again. "In fact, what he said was: 'If this new play of Barnaby's is as excellent as that *Airplane Story* of his, I'm certain the fifteen percent cut he's offering us will be sufficient to put us out of business. So, thanks, girl, but no thanks."

Bob was incensed by the insult. "That son-of-a—"

"Calm down, man," Lisa said soothingly. "It ain't the end of the world. Ignore Brody. He's so old-fashioned he still thinks Reagan is president. Let's just move on. You've got this new show and it's definitely a good one. I know shows and I've a great feeling about this *Marriages and Divorces*. I mean, your cast of performers are gonna knock it right out of the ballpark."

"I'm glad *someone* believes in me," Bob said glumly.

"I do, Bobby, I really do," Lisa said. "You just need to remain calm, that's all. Once premiere night is past and the theater critics' reviews are in, you'll have no problem at all finding backers. Liam Brody will come looking for you with dollar signs in his eyes."

That was encouraging talk to Bob. "You really think so?"

"Sure, I do. Hey, listen, speak to you later, man. Someone's knocking on my office door. I think it's the coffee and cream cake I ordered for brunch being delivered."

Bob felt better after she hung up. *Yeah, Lisa's right. All I've gotta do is hold on past tomorrow night and then we'll be back on top again. Nothing can go wrong now. Yeah!*

Then he realized that someone was knocking on the door of his office.

"Come in," he said.

The door opened and Case and Helen Miller entered.

The Millers were both in their late thirties and had apparently been in the theater all their lives. Case Miller was tall and gaunt, with cropped brown hair, while his wife was a shapely blonde. The Millers were playing the lead parts in *Marriage and Divorce* and were both wearing their stage clothes— Case was dressed in a blue pinstriped suit as if he'd just gotten home from the office, while Helen, who was playing the part of a suburban housewife, wore a purple sundress decorated with yellow flowers, and a blue apron as if she'd been busy in the kitchen.

The couple didn't look happy though, Bob noted as he gestured to the pair of chairs on the other side of his desk.

"What's the matter?" he asked once they were seated. "Fergie told me you guys were having a meeting downstairs. Is something wrong with one of the stage props?"

For a few moments neither of the Millers said anything, though husband and wife both darted furtive glances at one another as if urging themselves to go first.

Finally, Case cleared his throat. "Um, Bob, it's about our salaries..."

"Yeah," Helen agreed with a firm nod. "The cast and crew want to know when we're gonna be paid."

Oh no, not today of all days, Bob thought. He avoided looking at the ceiling of his office, but still prayed silently: *Oh dear God, please let this not be about what I think it's about.*

Then he put on his most insincere smile. "I don't understand. I though we'd already discussed this."

Case nodded. "Sure, we did. And you agreed to pay us yesterday. You said the bank was gonna advance you the money, remember?"

Of course, Bob remembered. How could he not remember? But he also remembered that he'd just gotten off the phone to Lisa and that Lisa had told him there wasn't going to be any salary money coming from the bank.

How best to break the bad news to the couple seated opposite him? Bob considered lying to them, but then decided that there was no point in doing so. The Millers and the rest of the cast were very loyal to the Barnaby cause. Bob knew everyone was broke now—hell, he was broke and penny-pinching himself—but they'd all agreed to stick it out and pull off *Marriage and Divorce*, which everyone was certain would put some money in their pockets again.

"Listen, guys, I got some bad news for everyone…"

Bob didn't like the way the Millers' eyes kept widening as he explained that there was no money coming from the bank. Nor did he like the anger that flared up in Helen's eyes when he pleaded with them to just hang on for one more day.

"Hey, guys, it's just until tomorrow night," he finished with a weak shrug. "Surely we can all hold out until then."

"Hold out?" Helen smirked pityingly at him. "Bob, that's easy for you to say. Case and I? Both of our credit cards are maxed out. We've both been eating nothing but ramen noodles for two weeks now."

Case nodded. "Yeah. At the moment I'm so hungry that I start salivating when I see roaches on the wall."

"I'm so hungry that instead of clouds I see burgers floating in the sky."

"Yesterday I looked at a dog turd on the sidewalk and it really looked like a hot dog."

"I'm so malnourished, I dropped two dress sizes in two weeks."

Bob knew the couple were exaggerating. "Oh, c'mon, guys, it's not that bad. I mean, I'm flat broke too—can hardly afford gas for my car, but like I said, after tomorrow night we'll all have some money and we can buy—"

"There won't be a tomorrow night if we don't get some money today," Helen said flatly.

Bob looked at her in surprise, then slowly turned to stare at her husband.

Case nodded back. "For real, man. That's what the meeting we were having was all about and what we came up to tell you."

Bob gaped at them both. "You guys can't be serious. Not after all the work everyone's put in. You can't just..." He fell silent because the stony looks on his companions' faces assured him that they were dead serious.

"Sorry, man," Case said. "We didn't mean for this to happen, but..."

"Jenny fainted during her scene," Helen said in a miserable voice. "When we roused her, she said she'd not eaten anything since yesterday morning." Helen glared at Bob, her eyes placing the blame for Jenny's faint firmly on his shoulders. "That's how hungry everyone is. And we're not about ruining our acting reputations by all dying on stage of malnourishment."

"So," Case said, "it's either we all get some cash right now, or you don't have a stage play tomorrow night."

"But I don't have any money to pay anyone!" Bob blurted out. "I just got through telling you about the bank's decision not to loan me any more money."

"Then you don't have a show tomorrow night," Case said flatly. "Sorry, Bobby, but it's not our fault. Everyone is in on this decision. We're just the messengers."

"Now, don't shoot us," Helen said in a mocking voice as she and her husband got up from their chairs. "All you gotta do is pay us and the show goes on."

***

That was all it took. Bob stood at the window of his office and watched everyone, both cast and crew, leave, all of them piling into the four cars available and driving off. No one looked back at him, no one looked up at his window. This upset Bob so much that he really considered leaping out headfirst from his window and breaking some of his bones in the front parking lot, just to make a point.

Once all the cars had driven off, Bob figured that just he and old Fergie were left in the building. He walked over to his desk and sat behind it, trying to work out exactly how, in less than an hour, things had collapsed around him.

CHAPTER 2

Old Dave Ferguson angrily shoved his mop ahead of him along the floor. He'd been downstairs when the abrupt staff exodus began and had heard everything everyone said as they left.

"Hey, you can't just leave like this!" he'd protested. "The kid needs you now."

"Tell that to my hungry stomach," Jenny, the girl who'd fainted, told Fergie in return and then strode past him, calling back over her shoulder: "Except Bob finds us some money by tomorrow morning, nothing is happening here!"

Fergie didn't know what to say. The kids had a valid complaint. Fergie hadn't been paid too. He however lived with his daughter and her husband, so he'd been alright in the interim, and Bob did slip him a few dollars every now and then to help tide him over till things normalized.

But Fergie's not quitting now had to do with more than just that. Fergie felt a deep connection to this old building. In fact, he felt more connected to the Barnaby Theater than its current owner did; the owners changed, the theater remained the same. Fergie had worked here since he was twenty-four and now that he was sixty-four, he didn't know what else he'd do if he quit like everyone else.

Fergie definitely wasn't looking forward to next year, when he'd be retiring, because that meant he wouldn't be working here in this building anymore.

But even that dreaded retirement date was much better than this; watching things fall to pieces before his very eyes.

"Damn, this is surely gonna end badly," the old man said, shaking his head as the troupe all streamed out the building, loaded themselves into their cars, and zoomed off.

He could almost hear the Barnaby Theater weeping and pleading with them all to come back and give it a chance to survive.

Oh yes, Fergie knew that the Barnaby Theater was in dire straits. He knew all about that loan that young Bob Barnaby had taken from the bank to finance *Airplane Story*.

I didn't approve of young Bob taking that dumb loan back then, but of course, I'm just the hired help. No one ever consults us before taking decisions.

Fergie also knew that it would soon be time for the bank to take full ownership of the building—which would mean he'd most likely be out in the cold without his beloved job.

Fergie had no illusions that the bank would continue to host dramas here.

Hell no, that ain't the modern way. The good old times when folks liked to leave their houses and gather and enjoy a good play together is almost gone. Now everything's cinema and even that's been fading for a while now. What's in fashion now is that Netflix streaming thing that my daughter and her teens keep watching on their laptops and smart TVs.

Fergie suddenly felt too tired to do any more cleaning. *What's the point? It don't look like anyone else is gonna be coming in here today.*

The old-timer wrung his mop and pushed the cleaning cart to one side against a wall, then he walked into the large amphitheater and sat in one of the middle seats facing the stage.

What the bank is sure to do once they own this place is sell the lot to some developer who's gonna tear the theater down and put up a McDonalds or other fast-food outlet in its place! And just like that, a huge chunk of neighborhood tradition is gonna be gone forever.

Fergie had been desperately hoping that this new play *Marriage and Divorce* that the drama troupe had been rehearsing would do the trick, would help Bob pay off his bank debts.

"It's a good play, a great play, and it'd have been a hit for sure," Fergie groaned aloud, banging fist against the back of the chair in front of him. "Everything would have been fine except that Jenny had to go faint during a dress rehearsal today. Couldn't the silly girl have waited till tomorrow to faint?"

But what was done was done.

"Oh, yes, this is certainly gonna end badly," Fergie said again.

CHAPTER 3

Saying that Bob Barnaby had no idea whatsoever of what to do now would be the understatement of the century.

For more than four hours after the drama troupe deserted the theater Bob sat in his office with his mind empty, trying to figure a way out of his dilemma. Bob's mind was so empty of constructive ideas that in all those long hours when he sat staring at the walls of his office it didn't occur to him even once to phone Lisa back and update her on what had transpired after her call.

"I have a good show," he repeatedly told himself out loud while shaking his head in stunned disbelief. "In fact, it's a GREAT show; a surefire hit for sure. All I need is money. But money is what I don't have."

The problem was that Bob had nowhere to look for money. He figured he needed about ten thousand dollars to keep his cast and crewmembers happy, but he had no one he could borrow the money from.

In the months since *Airplane Story* had tanked, he'd long exhausted all his borrowing options.

Of course, there were the illegal routes—he could visit a loan shark—but even though he'd sometimes felt suicidal over the past year, he didn't consider himself *that* suicidal. With the way his luck had been recently, he dreaded having to lose a finger or even a hand when his marker came up and he couldn't make good on it.

He got up and walked over the cabinet where, to celebrate miserable occasions such as this, he kept a bottle of whiskey. But even here he was to be disappointed. The whiskey bottle was empty. Bob rolled his eyes.

Hey, I'll go see Jane, he suddenly decided.

Jane worked as a waitress at the Black Bear Diner, just short walk west on Broadway, the same street that the theater was on. The two had so much in common: she was a theater fan and he would often drop by the Black Bear to grab a bite to eat.

She was on the morning shift today, which meant...Bob checked the time on his watch, it was now about four-thirty...yes, she should be back home now.

They were supposed to meet up tonight anyway, but Bob figured it didn't matter if he headed over there earlier. In his current state of mind, he hated being alone.

He sent Jane a quick text message: *Wanna come see u babe. U home?*

Her reply was equally swift: *Just got in. Sure, come over. What's d hurry?*

He typed, *Tell u when I get there*, sent it and put the phone in his pocket.

***

To Bob's relief his car started without any fuss. The battered old F-150 had been temperamental of late and Bob had no idea how long it would be before he drove it down to the scrapyard. But it worked for the moment; would get him over to Jane's apartment block. At the moment seeing her was all that mattered to him.

Jane is the sole anchor of stability I've got in this storm of craziness that's just enveloped me. I know that once I tell her how much of a mess I'm in, we'll be able to figure something out together

To be perfectly honest, Bob didn't honestly think that his fiancée Jane would have a solution to his problem, but he knew that just seeing her would make him feel a whole lot better.

***

In addition to her working there, Jane also lived over in Broadway Towers apartment complex, a short walk for her, considering that Jane currently didn't have a car. Her neighborhood was cheap, she didn't have a car, and Bob considered her current living conditions to be solely his fault.

If I'd been more successful she'd be living with me now.

But for the moment, considering the jointly miserable state of their joint finances, Jane's moving was totally out of the question. Her rent was reasonable, and although the building had a seedy vibe about it, Broadway Towers was also within easy walking distance of her waitressing job.

But still, as he parked his pickup truck behind the light blue van near the entrance of the apartment block, Bob couldn't help but wrinkle his nose in disgust at the sordidness of the surroundings. Even the folks around here looked run down.

Just like me, he thought. *No point judging them and thinking they're lazy; two days from now I'm gonna be one of them too...unless . . .*

He still didn't know what he was going to do. He had a smidgen of an idea in his mind, an idea that concerned Jane...*But, nah,* he cautioned himself, *no way will that actually work.* But still, his vague hope was better than nothing.

Bob got out of his car and locked it. While walking past the blue van he read the yellow lettering on its sides. 'Hobart's Elevator Services.'

Oh, my God, no, he thought, smacking his palm against his head as he walked over to the building's entrance. *I forgot that the elevator is busted.*

The high-rise's elevators had been problematic for a while now, and now that he thought about it, Bob remembered that the reason Jane was coming to see him tonight and not him visiting her, was because yesterday and today were the days that her building's elevators were scheduled for maintenance work.

Sighing, Bob stepped into the lobby and headed for the stairs.

Tenth floor coming up!

Climbing the first few floors was fine; but once Bob got past his accustomed limit of three floors, which was what the Barnaby Theater possessed, the ascent began to take a toll on him. He wasn't the only one on the stairs, but most folks who passed him were headed down and not up, which Bob already agreed was the more sensible direction to be traveling in.

Oh, I really need to exercise and diet more!

At the fifth floor, he stopped to rest, passing the time by staring out of the landing window at the neighborhood. On a normal day he'd have been criticizing its dinginess, but today he was too preoccupied with the question of his theater's survival to do so.

Okay, time to get moving again!

He ascended three more flights of steps and paused again on the eighth-floor landing. Just two more flights to go. But those two seemed like he was trying to gain access to Heaven itself. Most likely because of his worries, Bob was already completely winded. His brain ached from thinking. His legs ached from climbing. At the moment visiting Jane didn't seem such a smart idea at all.

But he'd already come too far to turn back. And Jane would be mad if he turned back.

So, Bob steeled himself and climbed the last two flights of stairs. Then, drenched in perspiration, he stood on the tenth-floor wheezing for breath.

Yes, for certain, I really do have to begin working out!

After about a minute's rest, he felt better and walked down the corridor to Jane's apartment.

CHAPTER 4

Jane had been waiting expectantly for Bob to arrive. On the phone he'd sounded worried, but she put that down to nerves. Tomorrow night was a big one for Bob—his clear chance to get back into the showbiz limelight—and anyone in his position would understandably have butterflies in their stomachs.

And then we can get married and I can leave this horrible neighborhood!

Jane had been standing by the window of her cramped living room, but now she turned away from the annoying view. She'd seen Bob's car turn the corner at the end of the street and then pull into the building's parking lot, and knew he was on his way up.

She was really looking forward to seeing him. Now they could spend the entire evening together.

Jane didn't envy him the climb though. She'd climbed those ten flights of stairs herself when returning from work an hour earlier. She giggled at the thought of Bob, who was definitely out of shape (something she definitely intended to fix once they were married), huffing and puffing as he climbed. Taking the stairs was easier for Jane. As a waitress, she was on her feet for hours each day and so had strong legs. Bob, on the other hand, sat in his office all day drinking coffee and occasionally going down to oversee his actors.

Jane detested living in Broadway Towers. These were built as housing projects by the city and quickly became a slum in everything but name. The residents of Broadway Towers consisted mainly of folks surviving with government assistance. It had a transient feel due to the high tenant turnover. She believed she deserved better from life.

Jane, who was a tall and slim blonde and a pretty and vivacious young woman, had grown up a poor country girl. Originally from Clarksburg, West Virginia, at the age of twenty she'd fled to the big city with dreams of becoming an actress.

She'd met Bob during her rounds of acting auditions. By then she was quite discouraged; but Bob had both encouraged her and put her on stage—a little part in one of his plays.

Only, poor Jane Piper had now discovered that, although she functioned perfectly okay during rehearsals, once faced with an actual audience, she was unable to act—she got stage fright of the worst possible kind: her body froze up and she forgot all of her lines.

As she'd weepily told Bob afterwards, "It seemed like my brain suddenly became scrambled eggs."

Jane had done everything she could to overcome her fears of performing, including seeing a psychiatrist, but nothing worked. She simply couldn't act on stage.

Disappointed, she'd accepted defeat and resigned herself to simply being Bob's wife, which she knew wouldn't be a bad thing. She loved Bob and he loved her and together...she dreamt of them having a big house and lots of happy, bouncy children.

And Jane had almost had all of that too. Except for that theatrical fiasco known as *Airplane Story*, she and Bob would have been happily married by now and would have started their family. But no, that horrible play had ruined everything for Jane.

Now, Jane walked over and sat in one of her armchairs, her brow furrowing up in thought as she relived her disappointment.

Just two weeks more and I'd have been a happy blushing bride and then . . .

Tears almost came to her eyes again at the memory.

Jane wanted a BIG 'showbiz' wedding. Though she couldn't be an actress herself, she wanted to get married like one, with a wedding dress fit for a empress, the paparazzi in attendance, light bulbs flashing in her face and a huge reception party with a giant cake. She wanted A-list theater and movie actors and actresses at her wedding and oh yes, she definitely wanted TMZ reporting it to the world. She wanted the whole shebang, period.

Jane had boasted to her two older sisters that she was going to have the most memorable wedding that had ever held in their family.

"Just you wait and see, girls," she'd told the two plump farmer's wives, "when Bob and I tie the knot we're gonna have the grandest wedding of all time.' "

Her mother had sighed. "Don't boast like that, dearie. It brings bad luck."

But Jane hadn't listened. She'd told everyone she knew in her tiny, glorified farmstead of a hometown that she was engaged to be married to one of the brightest lights in the theater world and that they were all invited to attend her wedding.

And then...and then that horrible *Airplane Story* had tanked and well...Jane hadn't been back to her hometown since.

After the play flopped and it was clear that her expected 'Grandest Wedding of All Time' would be happening anymore, Jane had immediately deactivated her Facebook and Instagram accounts. She'd uninstalled WhatsApp and any other messaging apps from her cellphone, and had begun screening and blocking all her calls, so that no one other than Bob, her employers, and her immediate family could contact her.

Her wedding dress (one fit for a queen in a Roman-themed drama) had already been ordered and Jane had wept a river of tears when she'd had to cancel the order for that magnificent work of tailoring and embroidery, and the bridesmaids gowns that accompanied it.

Jane sighed now as she watched the white ceiling. She ran her fingers across her forehead as if wiping away beads of sweat on this cool spring evening.

Oh, last year was a complete horror! But thankfully, Bob is about to produce another smash hit and we'll finally be able to get married.

Jane simply couldn't wait for tomorrow night's premiere of *Marriage and Divorce*. She intended to be in the front row of the audience, cheering along the play, and simultaneously cheering herself down the church aisle.

Oh, and God help anyone who got in the way of her marriage this time!

Then she frowned. *Hey, but where's Bob?* Jane figured that even someone as out-of-shape as her boyfriend ought to have reached the tenth floor by now. Her calculation was confirmed when she heard the sound of his key in the lock.

"Oh, darling," she said with delight in her voice, rising from the armchair and rushing over to welcome him with a kiss.

She could tell that something was wrong with him by the way he kissed her back. Normally his lips played passionately with hers, but now they felt dead and kissing Bob felt like kissing a frog...not that Jane had ever kissed a frog but she figured this must be how all those princesses in the fairy tales felt while kissing their transformed princes.

The feeling was so repulsive to Jane that she stepped away from Bob and now regarded him with worry.

Yes, something was definitely wrong here.

"Are you okay, honey?" she asked Bob as he plodded past her to lie flat on his back on the couch.

He shook his head. "I'm not sure if I'll ever be okay again."

Jane frowned. Now this was serious. She'd know Bob for four years now and he'd never looked this upset before, except when . . .

Her eyes widened and her lips trembled with fright. *Oh, no it can't be happening to me again. No, it's not fair! It can't be!*

Still, Jane managed to calm herself down, and she walked over to sit beside Bob on the couch. She stroked his sweaty face with a hand.

"What're you talking about, honey?"

Bob looked at her like he was about to start weeping. "Darling, you're not gonna believe this, but unless I can somehow pull off a miracle, the play's off."

Jane froze. This was even crazier than she'd suspected. "Off? How can it be off? Did the bank foreclose...no, they can't do that; you've still two months to go. So what?"

Bob covered his eyes with his left hand. "Everyone quit on me because they hadn't gotten paid."

"But...but...but...I thought the bank was going to...going to...I mean wasn't Lisa going to...?"

"Lisa spoke to Brody, but the old guy still won't budge an inch. And then..."

Jane listened in quiet disbelief while her boyfriend explained how Case and Helen Miller (she'd never liked that sneaky woman!) had walked into his office and issued an ultimatum, or else . . .

The staff walkout understandably had Bob looking devastated, but Jane felt worse. This news felt to her like the bottom falling out of her world...again. Jane had been dreaming of this new wedding she'd have, thinking how if she made it spectacular enough she'd be able to recover some of her lost glory in her hometown...and now . . .

She began weeping. She couldn't help herself.

"Oh, why is fate so unkind to me?" she moaned beneath her breath.

The tears ran from her eyes like twin waterfalls.

Bob sat up and tried to comfort her, but Jane shoved him away. Suddenly she was very angry with him. She began to see Bob in a brand-new light—this just had to be Bob's fault. Oh yes, Jane was certain it was, because if it wasn't, what was the statistical probability of her missing out on a big society wedding twice? Not once, but twice? She doubted she'd ever heard of it happening before. And if that wasn't Bob's fault, whose could it be? The Millers? No, not even Helen would stoop that low. Helen would realize how important a lavish wedding was to a girl.

While she'd been weeping and pondering her woes, Bob had moved in close to her to attempt comforting her again. His arms were wrapped around her, but Jane felt cold as ice.

"Listen, it's going to be alright," Bob said.

She could hear the lack of belief in his own voice and it made her laugh.

"Alright? How?" she asked angrily. And now that she thought of it, she realized that she was right: Case and Helen Miller were committed and dedicated actors; Jane didn't believe they'd quit a show so close to opening night. Which meant that...She glared at Bob.

"Hey, you're lying. The cast didn't quit. You fired them all."

Bob gaped at her. "Fired? Everyone? Jane, why in the hell would I go and do that?"

Jane was too angry to reply. Sure, Bob looked sincere, but then he'd always looked sincere. But now she could see right through him. It was crystal-clear to her now—Bob had fired the cast so he could get out of marrying her. He knew she wanted a grand wedding and he was simply too much of a cheapskate to fork out the required cash. No wedding meant no spending.

"You don't love me!" she shrieked at him. 'That's all this is really about. You don't really love me!"

She wept more fiercely; her shoulders jerking violently as she did so. Bob was speaking to her, but she barely heard what he said; her misery and displeasure were an emotional shield against his presence.

But then Bob said something that she did hear, something that froze Jane's tears and made her raving mad instead.

She jerked away from his embrace and glared at him in fury. "What did you just say? Repeat it, I didn't hear that too well."

Bob gulped and looked guilty as hell. "Well, I was thinking that there might be a way to salvage things."

"Which is?"

"Well, seeing as you used to be an actress, I was thinking that you could act the lead female role and I'll try to do the lead male—"

Jane slapped him. Then she leapt up and stormed across to the other side of the living room. Her intention was to find something that she could throw at Bob, but fortunately for him, her anger got the better of her before she made it to the shelves that held her potted plants.

She spun around and glared at Bob. "What, what, what!?"

"Sweetheart, it's only a suggestion. Yes, I know you've got that horrible stage fright, but this is an emergency. If I don't put on a play tomorrow night, I'm through."

Jane was incensed. *I can't believe my ears. Not only does this rat want to frustrate me; he also wants to embarrass me in front of everyone. He knows I'll make a complete fool of myself if I dare venture onstage and yet...*

The nasty revelation triggered a fresh burst of tears.

"Oh, come on now, darling," Bob said. "I know you don't like acting, but it's not *that* bad."

Jane shook her head. "Bob, I quit too."

Bob looked nonplussed but managed a smile. "Sweetheart, you can't quit. You don't work for me."

She stared pityingly at him. "Don't you dare call me 'sweetheart' ever again. And I don't mean I quit as your employee—I quit as your fiancée. We're though. Finished. Over...for good. Read my lips...get out of my life."

The shocked look that now came over Bob's features did make Jane wonder if she was misjudging him. But she was too angry to care.

"Listen, sweetheart, I think you're taking this a little bit too far," Bob said nervously, getting up from the couch and walking towards her.

"Don't you dare call me 'sweetheart!' " Jane thundered at him. "I'm not your damn 'sweetheart' anymore!"

"Sweetheart, please!"

Bob stopped coming closer when Jane picked up a potted plant from its place on a shelf.

"Get out of my apartment," she told him in a deadly voice.

"Please, sweet...please, Jane, listen to me."

Jane hefted the potted geranium over her head. "Get...out...now!"

Bob began backing away. Jane followed him at a distance. "Leave my house keys behind, you rat," she told him. "You aren't welcome here anymore."

Bob fiddled around in his pocket till he found his key ring, then he quickly separated the key to her apartment door from the rest and dropped it on the backrest of an armchair.

"Listen, darling, just gimme a chance to explain myself," he pleaded.

Jane shook the potted plant threateningly. "Don't call me 'darling' either. I'm not your 'darling' anymore." He was standing beside her front door now and she nodded towards it. Alright, now get outside and start walking, and don't you ever come back here again. I utterly hate you."

Bob opened the door. He looked really pitiful now. "But sweetheart, I mean, Jane...Darling, I still love you. I..."

"Shut up and go!" Jane launched the geranium through the air at him.

Bob ducked outside the apartment and got the door shut behind him just in time. A second later Jane's geranium crashed against the door, the impact shattering its clay pot and spraying sand everywhere.

Jane stood there glaring in rage at the door through which Bob had just fled, then she retreated to the couch, sat down on it and burst into tears again.

CHAPTER 5

Bob's ten-floor trip back downstairs passed very quickly. In addition to the fact that it's always easier to descend stairs than to climb them, the trip passed speedily because, throughout its duration Bob's mind was preoccupied with the question of which method of suicide would suit him best.

Jane just dumped me? It made no sense to Bob. He'd come here to offload his soul to the woman he loved and she'd...thrown him out of her house?

Bob was still numbed with shock. His bad day had just gotten terminally worse. So much worse in fact that Bob honestly now viewed death as a welcome alternative.

I'm about to lose my theater and I've just lost my fiancée...What the hell else have I got to lose? What am I living for?

But still the right method of suicide eluded him. There were obviously lots of ways to kill oneself nowadays, so many in fact that the modern would-be suicide was spoiled for choice:

A bullet to the head? Swift and in theory, painless. 'In theory' because, well, who'd ever survived being killed to testify to the truth of the assertion that gunshots to the brain didn't hurt? And there was also the additional consideration that shooting oneself in the head left a big hole and an even bigger mess.

Hanging? Hanging seemed overdone. And there were several morbid calculations to consider: apparently one had to get the height of the drop just right, or else the fall didn't break your neck like you'd intended and you swung there slowly choking to death, which would surely be very painful. There was also a mess involved; from what Bob had heard, suicides often wound up either wetting themselves or voiding their bowels. Yuck.

Slitting one's wrists? Also overdone, and also guaranteed to leave a mess (at least in the bathtub). But if the bathwater was warm, it was supposed to be a soothing way to exit this life. But just like in the case of shooting oneself in the head, who had ever survived their own death and, so, was qualified to give evidence?

Or maybe an overdose of sleeping pills was the way to go. Simply go to bed at night and not wake up the next morning. But exactly how many pills was one supposed to take? No problem there; the information had to be available somewhere on the internet.

With this matter of the perfect way to kill himself still unresolved in his mind, Bob stepped down from the stairwell and crossed the lobby to the front entrance.

As the building's front doors swung shut behind him, he checked his watch.

6:15 p.m. What the hell was he going to do with himself now?

He glanced around the neighborhood. There were more people on the streets now than when he'd arrived here. The elevator repairers' van was still parked in front of his car, but the workmen seemed to have finished their maintenance work; a group of three men in blue work overalls stood beside the van, along with three women in regular street clothes. The six of them were conversing, drinking sodas and laughing, and though Bob thought he also heard the sound of a couple arguing somewhere nearby, it clearly wasn't any members of this group beside the van.

Bob felt so bad already that the realization that the building's elevators were probably working again now, and he'd not needed to walk down the steps at all ran off his soul like water off a duck's back.

Seeing the workmen and their lady friends and hearing their happy male-female conversions made Bob sad. Barely an hour ago he'd had a girl too, a woman who'd loved him, and who'd pledged to stick with him through thick and thin.

And now, she's gone. Jane's left me.

The shock of Jane's desertion now fully hit Bob. And the pain of losing Jane was much worse than the mere fear that he'd lose everything he owned because his actors had quit. Bob choked back sobs and wiped tears from his eyes.

A truck was just turning the corner down the road. And seeing that the vehicle was headed his way—and was certain to pass in front of Jane's building—Bob determined to end his life right there and then.

All he had to do was step in front of the truck at the right moment and his life would be over. And then Jane—silly Jane who thought he'd staged his workers' walkout because he no longer wanted to marry her—would see how badly she'd wronged him.

Bob didn't really want to hurt Jane or make a point about anything. He was just tired of the downward turn which his life had taken. He'd been serious when he'd proposed that Jane attempt the female lead in *Marriage and Divorce* while he played the male one. True, there was no time for either of them to properly learn their lines, but the play itself was a satire on marital roles and it just might be possible for them to wing it, wing it at least until he found new actors who could learn the parts.

At this point it really didn't matter if the reviews sucked. The one thing Bob couldn't afford to do was not put on a show tomorrow. He'd already spent too much on sets and clothes and promotion; so much money that he couldn't cancel the performance even if he wanted to; he didn't have the money to put out additional notices that the play had been cancelled.

Best that I just cancel myself, he accepted with glum finality, crossing the parking lot with deliberate fast strides towards the sidewalk. The oncoming truck was really close now. Bob knew he had to time his leap out in front of the vehicle just right, or else the driver might swerve away in time and fail to kill him. It would be mortifying if all his suicide attempt resulted in was a broken arm or leg. Then all he'd have succeeded in doing would be to compound his problems with a compound fracture.

But then, as Bob stepped past the van belonging to the elevator repair crew, he happened to glance to his left.

Afterwards, Bob could never explain to himself what exactly made him glance that way at that particular moment.

The result of that glance however was that Bob halted his forward rush to throw himself in front of the oncoming truck, which rumbled harmlessly past.

And so it was that young and suicidal Bob Barnaby lost his chance to kill himself, but he found something else.

CHAPTER 6

What had arrested Bob's attention was the couple having an argument on the sidewalk, beside the elevator repair crew's van.

They were a young pair and the young man was clearly also one of the elevator repairmen—he was wearing the same blue coveralls as the workmen standing with the women on the van's other side. But while his companions looked like everyday workers, this kid looked like Elvis in his heyday; and his aggrieved girlfriend looked equally good, a sort of cross between Marilyn Monroe and Taylor Swift. Slim and with long blonde hair, she had on a pink top, white stretch pants and black pumps and looked like she'd just fallen out of a fashion magazine.

Bob was struck by the couple's good looks. And there was more that caught his eye about them. They had a striking vitality that was almost theatrical.

"Ha, that's what you always claim!" the girl was saying, waving her hands as if she was performing. "And, hear me, I don't believe you anymore. I'm warning you that the next time I see you with her I'm gonna—"

"You're imagining things, babe. I already told ya that there's nothing between us two."

The girl turned towards Bob then and Bob got the impression that he knew her from somewhere. But her identity was secondary; what was uppermost in his mind was the striking revelation that this pair would look perfect on stage. Even without rehearsing, they had the right gestures—the young brunette in particular was so theatrical in her actions that she could be a stereotype. And best of all, they shared a strange chemistry. There was just something extra-special about the combination of the two of them.

But they clearly have no theatrical experience, the sensible half of Bob's mind protested. *It'll be a complete disaster.*

It already is a complete disaster, he replied himself. *It can't get any worse than it is.*

Before he could convince himself to change his mind, Bob strode over to the arguing couple.

"Hello, both of you."

The pair turned at his approach. The young man had an irritated look on his face, while his girlfriend—yes, Bob definitely knew her from somewhere—glared angrily at him.

"What do you want?" she asked. "Can't you see that we're not in the mood to meet strangers?"

Bob cleared his throat nervously. "My name's Bob Barnaby, I run the Barnaby Theater across town, and I need actors for a play that I'm putting on there tomorrow night. You two look perfect for the part. I was wondering if you have any acting experience?"

"Ha!" the girl said. "Of course, we do! Ted here's been acting like he loves me for the past three years."

'Ted' scowled back at her. "Oh yeah? Well, Molly darling, each time you open that pie hole of yours I wanna hand you the Oscar for worst actress of the year. All you know is drama, drama and more drama. One would think you were raised in the theater."

"You can't talk to me like that," his girlfriend fumed, her voice rising to a level that alarmed several passersby. "I...I—"

Ah yes, Molly! Bob now realized where he knew her from. She was one of the waitresses at the Black Bear Diner where Jane worked. She was new there, which was most likely why she didn't recognize him too, but he'd noticed her a few times while picking up Jane from work.

"Boy, I've had more than enough of you," Molly growled at Ted.

"Please, please," Bob quickly interjected into the situation before it got away from him. "I'm serious here. I'm short-staffed for my new play and the pair of you look perfect to be my lead actor and actress. Can either of you act?" Then he realized that in this case acting ability was clearly a secondary consideration. What he actually needed was the two of them on stage, projecting this strange personal chemistry they shared at the audience. So he adjusted his question: "No forget that—you don't need to have been on stage before. What I meant to ask was, would you be willing to give it a try?"

With relief Bob saw that he had now their full attention. For the moment at least they seemed to have forgotten their argument.

"Huh?" Molly said. "Us? You want *us* to act? Act, as in, perform on stage?"

Bob nodded. "Yes, for real."

Molly looked at Ted. "What do you say, man?"

Looking even more like Elvis now, Ted scratched his chin. "Acting, huh? Yeah, I'm sure we could give it a try. My mom always says I should be on stage. I've always wanted to be on stage."

Molly gave Bob a curious look. "When's the play, man?"

"Yeah, and what's it about?" Ted added.

Bob shrugged. "The play's tomorrow."

"Tomorrow!?" Molly yelped. "Hey, don't we need rehearsals first?"

"Don't worry about that," Bob said quickly. "The story is simple enough. You'll just ad-lib most of your lines. And to answer Ted's question—the play is called *Marriage and Divorce*. It's about the joys and travails of being a modern couple."

"*Marriage and Divorce,* eh? I like that," Molly said, giving her boyfriend another aggrieved look. "I wanna be married, but Ted here is too much of a chicken to make a real commitment to me."

Thankfully, Ted's mind was clearly taken up with another question:

"Hey, dude, how much are you gonna pay us to do it?"

Bob frowned; now they'd reached the difficult part of the negotiations. He clearly had no money, so he bluffed. "Oh, you'll get standard union rates. Yes, standard union rates." He figured he'd figure out another excuse when payday came, if it ever did.

His answer seemed to satisfy Ted and Molly.

"Okay, we'll do it," Ted said. He glanced at his girlfriend. "Right, baby?"

She nodded enthusiastically. "Yeah, we will."

"Hey how about us?" a gruff male voice said from behind Bob. "We wanna be actors too."

"Yes, we do!" a female voice agreed.

Bob turned around and saw that the rest of the elevator repair crew and their girlfriends or wives had joined them. Bob gave them a quick once-over—three guys, three ladies. The play had a cast of eight, and right here he had eight people. If he employed them all he no longer had to look for the rest of his cast.

Yippee, I'm saved. I'm saved!

"Okay, you're all part of the show," he told them all.

This pleased everyone and while the young women grinned at each other, the guys high-fived themselves.

"Okay, time to get to work," Bob said. "Let's head over to the theater for a brief rehearsal, so I can hand you all copies of the scripts and I can fill each of you in on your parts and what you gotta do on stage."

That said, everyone piled in the car and van and drove off together.

CHAPTER 7

Old Ferguson gaped in surprise when Bob walked into the Barnaby's amphitheater followed by a group of four workmen and four women.

"You aren't about breaking up the sets yet, are you?" he asked Bob worriedly, after pulling him aside while the others headed for the stage. "Don't do it, son; the Millers might relent and bring everyone else back."

Bob laughed. "Don't worry, Fergie. They're not here to break up the set." "They're my new cast."

Fergie gestured down the aisle at the eight people who'd accompanied Bob into the theater, and who were now standing by the front row seats and staring up at the stage. He stared at Bob in shock. "Those lot? Son, those look like blue-collar workers and waitresses to me. None of that lot look like they've ever acted a day in their lives."

Bob shrugged. "They haven't. I've got"—he glanced at his watch—"I've got exactly twenty-six hours to make stage performers out of them."

Fergie nodded speechlessly and watched Bob hurry down the center aisle to join his waiting 'cast,' who immediately crowded around him with eager expressions on their faces.

"Oh, my dear God, this is certainly gonna end badly," Fergie said with a sad look on his face.

CHAPTER 8

"Alright," Bob said once he'd assembled his impromptu cast up on the stage, "at this first rehearsal, I'll need to explain some theater basics to you all..."

He spoke and they listened raptly, like little children being told a bedtime story.

They truly were a motley crew—three couples and a pair of siblings. In addition to Ted and Molly, the others were Louie and Tess, Rhonda and Barry, and the brother/sister pair of Joe and Linda.

"Okay, now, for most of the play, the guys will enter from stage left, and the girls from stage right. I mean from the audience's point of view..."

While explaining about their stage positioning, Bob looked them all over. Louie, the leader of the elevator repair crew, was small and stocky and had cropped brown hair; his girlfriend Tess was a tall and thin blonde with an aggressive look to her. Rhonda and Barry were a married couple, both in their early thirties, both slightly overweight and both possessing long brown hair. Joe and his sister Linda both had black hair; Joe was tall, Linda was short.

The men of course were wearing their work clothes. The girls all dressed similarly, in tee shirts and denim pants or skirts, sneakers or boots. Rhonda and Tess had on fabric jackets.

There was an unpolished feeling to this whole ensemble that Bob just knew in his bones would transfer well to the stage.

"So, Louie, you enter there...yes, like that, but walk a bit slower, and then you stand there, by that pillar. Good, good, but don't look at me. You've got to look at Tess. You got that, man?...Good. Now, before Tess enters, you've been...Hey, I forgot to bring out the scripts. Hold on a bit and I get the scripts for all of you."

Aware of the excitement amongst his new cast, Bob quickly hurried offstage and fetched the scripts from their storage cabinet in the wings.

"Alright, here you go, everyone," he said as he handed them around.

"Wow, man," Rhonda said, waving the thick sheaf of papers at him. "This sure is a lot. There's no way we're ever gonna memorize all of this before tomorrow."

"Yeah," Ted said, with the others nodding.

"Man, you gotta be kidding us," Linda said. "I don't even like reading the menus at my waitressing job."

"Me neither, dude," her brother Joe agreed. "And this is like a hundred times that long."

"Just looking at all these pages is giving dyslexia," Louie added.

Bob shook his head. "Okay, don't try to remember any of it," he said soothingly, aware that he needed to build up everyone's confidence. They had to feel like this was all a joke; something they could easily accomplish.

"Look, guys, all you all gotta do is just try to get a feel for the story and who your character is supposed to be; that way once you step on stage, you'll be able to make up things as you go along. But always remember, the play is titled *Marriage and Divorce*, so all your made-up dialogue must hinge on that. Everyone got that?"

Nods all around.

"Good, so Ted and Molly, you two will be handling the two lead parts of Mr. and Mrs. Jackson. Louie and Tess, you'll be the Henningtons, the banker who's afraid his wife is cheating on him with his older brother, and his alcoholic wife who thinks he's on the verge of divorcing her....While, Rhonda and Barry you're the O'Reily's, the couple who run the bar....Linda and Joe, you two are playing the newlywed Clintons...and yeah, you two are brother and sister, so just leave out the kissing scenes, before we're accused of promoting incest..."

Everyone laughed.

"Okay now, everyone take fifteen minutes to read through the parts that you're performing and study your characters, and then we'll do a dry run. While you're all reading, I'll fetch the microphones and mic you all up, and turn on the sound too."

Bob had intentionally paired the natural couples together. It had been the same approach the Millers had taken, and one that he hoped with utilize the natural chemistry that bonded the pairs.

As he hurried up through the ramped central aisle to the sound booth, he realized he still had three problems to solve: Firstly, he needed to get a sound engineer to man the audio booth, and he also needed some stagehands. And third, he also needed someone in the wings to prompt the actors on their lines when they forgot what they were supposed to do or say.

But those are minor issues, things I can tackle tomorrow. What's important tonight is getting everyone into the spirit of the performance.

He paused at the top of the aisle, having just remembered something else.

Oh yeah, and I need to call Lisa, and let her know about this messy state of affairs. But, I'll do that tomorrow morning. No point in alarming her tonight.

***

"So, let me get this right, baby," Ted asked Molly in his deep and rich voice. "You're saying that you love me, but that sometimes you hate me too? Sorry, darling, but how is that even possible?"

Molly sighed, her amplified voice thin yet full of determination. "I dunno, I think it's just the way us girls are wired. All I know is, when I'm pleased with you, I'm very, very pleased with you and want to make you happy in every way that I possibly can...and when I'm mad at you, I wish I'd never met you and I also wish murder was legal."

"Hey, that ain't in the script," Tess instantly objected, waving hers at Bob. "The two of them just made all that up."

Bob raised his hands to call a halt. This was going better than he expected.

"Yes, it isn't in the script," he agreed. "And that's the whole point I'm trying to get across to you all." He gestured around the empty hall. "Just go with the flow. Have *real* conversations with one another; say what you feel like saying; just as if you were talking to each other at home or out on the street where I met you all." Then he wagged a cautioning finger. "Hey, but don't get dirty. Some innuendo is fine, but absolutely no four-letter words; as in, none at all please—it's not an X-rated show." He waved to Ted and Molly. "Carry, on please. You're both doing great."

Ted nodded to Bob and then, once more back in character, he turned and frowned at Molly. "For real, darling? You often feel like killing me?"

She giggled. "Yeah, honey, lots of times I do, but then I decide to just kill you with kindness."

"Hey, that there is just great," Bob enthused. "Guys, we gotta use that in the show tomorrow....Linda, you look like an army secretary. You're in charge of keeping notes of things like this; keep your cellphone on record all through the rehearsal, in case we come up with more great stuff like this."

Linda stiffened like a soldier at attention, raised her hand to her temple and saluted. "Gotcha, lieutenant!"

The rehearsal went on. Bob didn't even realize till much later that he'd been so wrapped up in work that he'd forgotten all about Jane.

But that indeed proved to be the case. After a while, he didn't even remember that she'd just broken up with him. The enthusiasm and desire to make this rescue project succeed completely overwhelmed him, and when they ended the rehearsal at 10 p.m. that night, Bob could say he felt quite optimistic about the future.

Well at least he felt he'd make it through tomorrow night's premiere okay.

CHAPTER 9

The next night, Jane arrived at the Barnaby Theater at 9 p.m.

Still mad at Bob and convinced of the rightness of breaking off her relationship with him, Jane had nonetheless come over to see if what he'd claimed was true, if his cast actually had quit on him.

That's proven easily enough, she thought after directing the Uber to drop her off a few blocks away from the theater. *If I arrive there and the place is deserted...but no, that doesn't prove anything—I still firmly believe that Bob fired everyone just to spite me!*

Once she'd alighted from the Uber, Jane felt even more annoyed. Bob clearly hadn't fired his actors at all. The show was still happening. The theater parking lot was filled with cars, with more pulling in as she walked towards the place. These were the latecomers; the show was scheduled to begin at 8:30. Jane had timed her arrival here for 9 p.m. to ensure she didn't run into Bob, who, once the stage performance got underway was certain to be preoccupied with supervising everything.

Growing more enraged with Bob by the second, Jane entered the building.

The ticket girl and ushers knew she was the boss's fiancée and waved her through. However, once past the foyer, Jane didn't enter the main theater hall where the play was being performed, but instead went through the right-hand side door that led backstage.

It took her a while to find Dave Ferguson. The old man was mopping up a disgusting puddle of something that both looked and smelt like puke. He and she were standing in the corridor that led to the ladies' dressing rooms and although Jane couldn't see the stage from here, she could hear someone speaking and the audience laughing.

"Thank God you came," Fergie whispered to Jane. "Your boyfriend has gone crazy."

Jane could care less about Bob's craziness. "Thank God he isn't my boyfriend anymore then," she angrily replied the old man and then pointed down at the puddle he was mopping up. "What happened?"

Fergie shook his head. "One of the new girls got stage fright."

Someone said something out on the stage then that caused the audience to burst into laughter, and next a man and a woman whom Jane didn't recognize ran out of the left stage entrance/exit into the vestibule where the actors sat until they were needed onstage again.

"Hey, who are those guys?" she asked Fergie. "I don't think I've seen them before."

"They're the new guys I just told ya about. Didn't Bob tell you that everyone quit on him yesterday?"

Jane stared at Fergie in surprise. "Yeah, he did, but I didn't think...I mean, I thought...I..."

"You don't love me in the least, you damn rat!" shrilled a female voice from out on stage. "You just say that because I'm gullible enough to believe it!"

"What on earth do you mean, woman? I'm always sincere with you."

"Don't you dare call me 'woman,' you patronizing man!"

"You are a woman, aren't you?"

"Not that sort of a woman! I'm not a 'woman' woman like you're inferring!"

"So, what should I call you then?"

"Oh, don't worry, darling," the unseen speaker acidly replied. "I'm certain you'll think of something as equally nasty as 'woman.' You always seem to."

A lot of female laughter now filled the air.

"Hey, I know those voices!" Jane told Fergie. "But it's impossible—what on earth would those two be doing on stage here?"

And before Fergie could reply, she dragged the old man down the corridor and into the vestibule, where they both peeked out at the actors.

Now Jane really didn't believe her eyes. *It was* Ted and Molly out there on stage.

What the hell is going on? she wondered.

As though he'd just returned from work, Ted was dressed in a navy-blue suit and was carrying a briefcase, while Molly, who sat in a chair and was exaggeratedly fanning herself with a Chinese fan, wore a white sundress with a rainbow pattern around its lowest portion.

Jane couldn't see much of the audience, but this premiere was well attended, and no one seemed bored yet. At the moment, Ted was opening up a fridge and taking out a beer, which he opened up and raised to his lips, while Molly watched him with a sneer on her beautiful face.

"Oh yes, that sure hits the spot after a hard day pretending to work," he said, provoking some laughter from the audience. "You know, honey, I used to work harder than I do now. But I discovered my boss prefers it when just I act hard like I'm working."

"Oh, give me a damn break," Molly said, fanning herself even harder.

"How the hell did they get out there...I mean, in here?" Jane whispered to Fergie.

"The boss brought them back here last night. Said he'd found them outside your place and they looked the part."

Jane gaped at the old man. "Looked the part? Is Bob crazy?"

"Sure, seems that way to me, girl."

"Listen, babe, don't give me the cold shoulder now," Ted told Molly. "You know I love ya!"

She smirked at him. "Oh yeah? So, if you love *me*, why d'you keep texting with Josie then? Lately it seems like you gotta text her for her opinion even before you kiss me."

"Babe, babe, please...you told me to get close to your baby sister! You're the one who said you want us to be friends, not enemies."

"Hey, man, I didn't mean you should get *that* close."

With a resigned look on his face, Ted turned towards the audience and addressed them. "See here, the trouble with you ladies is this—try to say what you mean and mean what you say. You want us guys to buy pizza and cokes for your younger sisters, cool, say so. You don't want us to do it, that's cool too. But make up your damn minds!"

The women in the audience were outraged. Boos filled the air.

"Yeah whatever," Ted told them.

"Hey, jerk," Molly yelled at him. "You're supposed to be talking to me, not to them.

Ted turned back to face her. "Yeah, babe, you're right. Now, where was I? Yeah, so you want me to be like how close to Josie?"

Still fanning herself, Molly got to her feet. "You really want me to spell it out for you?"

"Nah, babe, how 'bout if I get you a ruler and you measure it out in inches instead? That do for ya?

The men burst into laughter. The women booed some more.

"Are you certain that they're just acting?" Jane worriedly asked Fergie. "This is how the pair of them sound in real life. No one except themselves knows what they see in themselves."

And now, Molly began giving as good as she was getting. "You know what the problem with men is, man?"

"No, what?"

"You all act like the female heart is the engine of your car, something you can fix with a screwdriver. Well it doesn't work like that. Well, at least mine doesn't." She turned to face the women in the audience. "Hey, girls, do your hearts work like machines?"

Loud screams of "Hell no!" and "Of course they frigging don't!" filled the theater, with the ladies up in the gallery screaming to be heard above those in the main hall.

"Hey, that ain't fair," Ted protested. "You women are all ganging up on me."

"Turnabout's fair play, hon. I didn't complain when you got everyone involved. Now the shoe's on the other foot and you can't take the heat. Well, if you can't stand the heat, you know what they say, don't you?"

Ted looked miserable and aggrieved. Molly once again addressed the audience. "Hey, everyone, what's the right thing to do if you can't stand a woman's heat?"

"Get out of the kitchen," everyone shouted, the raucous mixture of male and female voices echoing through the building.

Jane turned to stare at Fergie in horror. "Wow, this is a real mess," she said. "The theater critics are gonna murder Bob over this"

"Yeah, I know," the old man said sadly. "This is certainly gonna end badly."

CHAPTER 10

Jane and Fergie's shared observation that Bob had just committed theatrical suicide was shared by Bob himself.

At the moment the owner of the Barnaby Theater was hiding in his office, too scared to remain downstairs and watch the show he'd produced. Once the curtain had lifted for the start of the show, Bob had told his stagehands he'd be back shortly…but then ran off to crawl beneath the metaphorical rock.

Oh, my dear God, I'm so done for right now, he thought on hearing the loud, unmistakable chorus of jeers and boos rising from the ground floor, then poured himself yet another round of whiskey from the giant bottle of Southern Comfort that he'd thoughtfully purchased earlier in the day. *Oh, but it seemed like such a great idea yesterday!*

More loud boos rose from downstairs; this chorus of disdain unmistakably female.

Bob took a huge gulp of whiskey to calm himself. He'd bought the bottle to celebrate his escape from the brink of disaster, but now that the disaster was clearly complete, drinking would surely be the only escape he'd have.

Oh heck, and Lisa did warn me against this!

Yes, Lisa *had* warned Bob. This morning he'd called her and told her everything that had happened yesterday. She'd immediately driven over to see for herself. She'd met Bob's new cast of workmen and waitresses rehearsing with gusto, exaggerating everything they did like the novices they were. She'd watched them making complete fools of themselves for four or five minutes and then, literally terrified by their thespian incompetence, had found an opportunity to pull Bob aside for a private conference.

"You can't use amateurs in a production of this importance," she'd insisted. "You're going to utterly ruin yourself."

Lisa Manning was a small woman in her late forties, with short black hair and piercing blue eyes. Very well-preserved for her age, Lisa always dressed conservatively like the lawyer she was; at the moment she wore a dark pantsuit over a peach colored blouse. She'd been frowning all the while, her lips pursed tightly together in displeasure, her eyes showing her disdain for Bob's so-called 'stage rescue team.'

"I'm already ruined," Bob had insisted back. "There's no other way out for me."

They'd both sat watching Bob's 'actors,' who were still reading from their scripts, though Bob had repeatedly told them not to worry about the actual words that they'd be saying; they could prompt each other all they liked and say whatever they wanted on stage, so long as it related to the idea of marriages and divorces—what was important was that they captured the spirit of the work.

"They're atrociously bad," Lisa had pointed out. "And except for your two leads, none of them are ever gonna win any awards for comeliness or personal grooming. Just look at the five-o-clock shadow on that Louie guy; hasn't he ever heard of an electric razor? And that girl—the one on the right who looks like she's related to that guy standing by the armchair..."

"You mean Linda? Yeah, you're right bout the resemblance—Joe's her older brother. What's the problem with her?"

"Bob, use your eyes. If Linda keeps widening hers like that each time she says something she considers witty, her eyeballs will soon pop out of her face. Her teeth are atrocious too, like she lives on a staple diet of chocolate, chocolate and more chocolate. And that other plump guy, Barry; his gestures are so wooden he could sign up to work as a fence post."

"Yeah, they're bad," Bob had admitted, Lisa's unwavering criticism seeding the first doubts into what had so far been an equally unwavering belief that he'd made the right decision by employing the elevator repair crew and their women yesterday.

"But you can see for yourself how committed to the project they are; I mean, all of them—*all* of them—took the day off from work today so they could be in the show." He sighed. "Actually, I'm counting on them being so bad that they're good."

Lisa had given him a pitying look. "Man, be serious, you're too experienced for that line of B.S."

"Well, what else can I do? At the moment I can only pray they're able to pull of something approaching a successful performance."

"Hey, come on, it's not that bad," Lisa had said. "You can postpone the show for a week. I'll ask around, see if I can get anyone to fill in for your cast and crew."

But while Lisa was a good friend and Bob understood that she just wanted what was best for him, he could read in her eyes that she herself understood the futility of her own advice.

"C'mon, Lisa, you're my lawyer," he'd said. "We both know the score here. I can't cancel this opening night, not at this late stage. I've sunk too much money into the project. If I hold the show tonight, before anyone knows how bad it is, I'll at least recoup some of the money spent on production costs, at least enough to pay the cast and ushers, the sound guy, and the two guys I got to help me with the stage props."

Lisa had nodded dryly at the stage, where, while Bob's impromptu cast rested between acts, two overweight men named Ollie and Jerry were rolling in a fake wall inset with windows and a door to block off the back of the stage. "Yeah, where'd you find those guys? Walmart?"

***

And now, it sounded like all of Lisa's predictions had come true. Thankfully, the whiskey had dulled the suicidal edge of Bob's thoughts, or else, with his window so close by, he might have considered plunging out through it head-first.

But even the booze couldn't hide the truth from him. *Marriage and Divorce* had just tanked worse that *Airplane Story* had; and where flopping was concerned *Airplane Story* had to be considered really big shoes to fill.

And of course, worst of all, Jane had left him too. He got up from his desk and walked over to his office window and stared down at the theater parking lot with its array of cars.

Ah, Jane, love of my life; why'd you desert me now when I need you the most?

Another thunderous chorus of jeers and boos rose up though the theater and filled Bob's head. He glanced at his watch. Just fifteen more minutes and his torment would be over. He had no idea what he'd do tomorrow; making it through tonight would be bad enough.

Aw well, at least I'll be able to pay everyone their 'standard union rates' like I promised.

Then his phone rang. "Who the hell is calling me now?"

He walked over to his desk and picked the phone up. *Oh, it's Lisa. What does she want?*

But it was obvious why Lisa, who was down with the rest of the audience watching the debacle Bob had 'produced' was calling him. "She just wants to rub it in my face!" he said angrily.

He was about to throw the phone out of the office window, but then changed his mind. Suddenly he didn't care. "Yeah? So, let her mock me."

So, he accepted the call. "Yeah, yeah, I know— you told me so. Now please let me drink myself to death in peace."

Even in his drunken state, however, he was unable to mistake the excitement in Lisa's voice. "No, no, no, don't hang up, Bobby. The play's a hit! Everyone loves it! You gotta come downstairs right away."

"I can't," Bob protested, "I'm half-drunk. I'll fall and break my neck on the stairs." The meaning of Lisa's words hadn't yet fully gotten through to him. All he could think about was how wobbly his legs suddenly felt.

"Okay, wait in your office and I'll come fetch you," Lisa said and then for the first time, unfiltered by the intervening theater walls, Bob realized that he could hear loud applause mixed in with the jeering and booing.

Three minutes later, Lisa was upstairs. "It's a hit!" she proclaimed in delight as she burst into his office. "*Marriage and Divorce* is a huge hit!" In her excitement she grabbed Bob and kissed him full on the lips, then she picked up his empty whiskey glass, refilled it and took a drink too.

Bob was too tipsy to care about Lisa kissing him, but her enthusiasm was infectious—it was slowly sinking into his brain that he was a success again.

Lisa got up and took his arm. "C'mon, let's get downstairs! The play is almost over and everyone is gonna want to meet the actors and producer!"

Bob allowed Lisa to lead him to the door. He felt saddened that it was Lisa and not Jane here with him now at this moment of unexpected triumph.

But what the heck, like they always say: the show must go on!

Bob grinned and grabbed Lisa, and, caught up in the euphoria and excitement of the moment, he kissed her on the lips too. Then they hurried downstairs together to bask in the glory of holding a successful premiere.

CHAPTER 11

For Bob, who since the days of the *Airplane Story* debacle had become used to being considered a third-rate player in the acting industry, the next few days passed in a sort of trance, a wonderfully delirious whirlwind.

According to the theater critics, all of whom were unanimous in their rapturous acclaim of the play, "With its built-in shattering of the 'third wall' barrier between performers and audience and the continuous interaction between them, *Marriage and Divorce* has set new standards in modern drama, a welcome change to the stifling and repetitive Shakespearian and Petrarchan tropes one is daily forced to consume in stage presentations.'

The feminist press were even more glowing. "Finally, here's a show where women can actually speak their minds without fear. *Marriage and Divorce* is a welcome breath of fresh air in the stale confines of male-dominated stage performance, a refreshing rainfall in the desert of patriarchy. Although clearly inexperienced on-stage Molly Baker brings a wonderful vigor and vitality to her performance that puts many a seasoned theater A-lister to shame. It doesn't hurt that she's beautiful too. The skill with which Ms. Baker and her Elvis lookalike co-star Ted

Miller constantly change the serious topics they satirize during each night's performance is a delight to behold."

But the best acclaim of all came from Harold Harrison, theater arts critic for the Tucson Times and a man whose opinion was considered the final word in the world of stage performances: "Bar none, these are the best actors that ever lived and their peers would all do well to emulate them," Mr. Harrison declared to friends at an after-show dinner, and later also wrote in his editorial column.

While the esteemed Mr. Harrison's praise for the cast of *Marriage and Divorce* was clearly hyperbolic and also heavily influenced by the amount of alcohol in his system at the time (an amount well over the state's drunk-driving limits and which got him pulled over by the highway patrol and subjected to a Breathalyzer test later that night), his words were nonetheless picked up by all his peers and trumpeted far and wide, from New York to L.A, up north to Boston and Chicago and down south-east to Miami.

After this, whether mockingly or seriously, everyone began referring to Ted, Molly, and the rest of the cast of *Marriage and Divorce* as 'The Best Actors That Ever Lived.'

There was no going down after that. Everything was up, up, up and away!

CHAPTER 12

Bob sat in his office mentally counting how much money he was now making. It was a lot.

Chair pushed back against the wall, feet crossed up on his desk, Bob grinned broadly. The scuffed state of his shoes no longer bothered him. He'd simply not had time to buy himself a few new pairs. Same with his clothes and everything else he needed to purchase or replace. He had no time to attend to such things; he was too busy attending to things in the theater.

This was better even than the good old days when he'd just taken over running the Barnaby Theater. *Marriage and Divorce* was now a nationwide sensation and on the verge of becoming an international one.

Oh yeah! I just knew Ted and Molly had that necessary intangible 'something.' I don't know how they keep improvising like that night after night, but it's incredible to watch.

Everyone else clearly agreed too. For the past six days they'd had sold-out shows, with crowds lining up around the block to get in even during downpours.

And the money. That was easily the best part of once more being successful. Old man Brody at the bank was now once more happily returning Bob's phone calls; and he had agreed that yes, projected on this new show's earnings—which were of course being paid into *his* bank's coffers—Bob would definitely be able to repay the loan he'd gotten by mortgaging the theater.

So, everything was fantastic on the financial front. And there was more money on the horizon. Lisa had already gotten offers from Broadway to put on a version of the play if it wasn't possible to bring the cast out to New York on such short notice. And in the theater world Broadway was the Big Time; big money time!

But remembering Lisa made Bob remember Jane also, and his delight immediately soured. Jane was the single black spot in all of this great success which Bob and the theater were currently enjoying. Just like he had on the night of the show's premiere, Bob wished she was the one by his side sharing his success and not Lisa.

He understood that he was being unfair to Lisa. Lisa was wonderful and she'd stood beside him when Jane had meanly kicked him out of her life. But his heart simply refused to agree with his head. Bob had no problem with Lisa being thirteen years older than he was. And it was clear that with her by his side the sky was the limit; showbiz people were already dubbing them 'the new power couple,' which Bob thought was very premature, seeing as he'd not yet 'coupled' with Lisa; not because she was unwilling to, but because each time he kissed Lisa he kept being tormented by visions of Jane, and he had the feeling that by going to bed with Lisa he'd be unfaithful to Jane. Which he knew was silly:

Dude, she doesn't want you anymore. She said she never wants to see you again! The two of you are through; try to get over it.

Thinking that way didn't help; didn't help one bit. Visions of Jane endlessly scrolled before him— Jane waving at him, Jane handing him a cup of coffee in the morning after he'd spent the night at her place, Jane smiling because he'd told her how much he loved her, Jane frowning because he hadn't told her how much he loved her, Jane serving tables at her waitress job, Jane walking home hand-in-hand with him. Jane in the swimming pool and so on and so forth.

The visions tormented Bob with their memories of all the happiness that he'd once had and had now lost.

Bob didn't get it; he really didn't understand how he could still be so obsessed with Jane even now that he knew the sort of selfish woman she really was. Particularly now when he was meeting lots of beautiful starlets and showgirls who kept giving him the eye, letting him know that they were his for the asking. But Bob just didn't feel like asking.

Damn, I'm going crazy. Maybe I need a drink.

But after glancing at the cabinet that held his trusty whiskey bottle, Bob shook his head. It was just noon, much too early in the day to get sloshed. He wasn't an alcoholic.

He folded his hands behind his head and did his best to push Jane out of his mind, trying to instead concentrate on the sounds coming from the street outside the theater, the everyday noises of traffic and the snippets of conversation from those walking past the house. He imagined he could hear some of those passing by talking about how he'd miraculously pulled the old neighborhood, with the theater as its centerpiece, back from the brink of disaster.

That didn't work either. Thoughts of Jane continued to plague him.

If she'd just call and say she that she was merely worked up and didn't mean it, I'd take her back immediately. I'll even speed up our wedding plans, we'll get married next weekend and...and...But...should I actually take her back? If Jane apologizes to me now, won't it just be because I'm now successful again?

These were sobering thoughts. Bob felt trapped between a rock and a hard place. He felt damned if his ex stayed away and equally damned if she didn't stay away.

He was saved from this depressing train of thought by a knock on the door.

"Come in," he called out.

His star actors, Ted and Molly walked in.

"Ah, just the people I wanted to see," Bob said with delight, taking his feet down of the desk and standing up to greet them. "Oh, you two were incredible last night. You just keep getting better and better. No one believes that none of you guys had ever done a day's acting before I discovered you outside Jane's place."

"Yeah, dude," Ted said dully, ignoring Bob's outstretched hand. He and Molly took the seats opposite Bob's.

Bob had no idea why both of his stars seemed so upset this morning. However, they soon enlightened him.

"We want to quit," Molly said.

"Yeah, dude, we can't do this anymore. We wanna stop being actors and return to our everyday lives again."

"Quit? Why? But...?" Bob ran out of words and just stared at the duo. And then a memory came to him and along with a sickening sense of déjà vu, he felt a cold shiver leaping up and down his spine like a monkey on amphetamines. This was exactly how it had happened barely a week ago—Case Miller had been sitting in the same chair that Ted was sitting in now, and Helen Miller in the once currently occupied by Molly.

"Hey, what's going on here?" Bob asked finally, his voice tiny and worried as he could see all the success of the past week evaporating right before his eyes. "Why in the world do you wanna quit the most successful stage show on the planet at the moment? You guys are being hailed as the best actors that ever lived, for chrissakes!"

Molly, usually the life of the party, sighed heavily. "It's just too *nasty*, that's why."

Bob was flabbergasted. "What? Nasty? Molly, it's just a play!" Then an angry thought knocked on the walls of his brain. "Hey, this isn't about the Millers threatening you guys in some way, is it? Because if they have been, I'll have the cops on them as fast as lightning."

Since the incredible success of *Marriage and Divorce*, Case and Helen Miller had been repeatedly calling Bob, and when he refused to reply their calls, later texting him pleading for forgiveness on behalf of the original cast. They wanted a second chance and were even ready to work for reduced wages.

But Bob wasn't having it; he wisely wanted nothing to do with the Millers anymore. He'd instructed Liam Brody to pay the betraying cast and crew their wage arrears. And once that was done, they were a burnt bridge. He'd already instructed the newly employed security guard at the entrance not to let them into the building under any circumstances.

The Millers' groveling behavior had once more made Bob suspicious of any attempts at reconciliation on Jane's part. One thing was certain however: Bob wasn't about to make the first attempt to reunite with Jane. And since she'd neither called nor texted him since the day she'd kicked him out of her apartment, so be it.

Good riddance to bad…only, no matter how hard Bob tried to think badly of Jane, he couldn't consider her 'rubbish.'

But back to his current problem. He stared at Ted and Molly in horror. "So have the Millers been hassling you guys to quit the show like they did?"

Ted shook his head. "Nope. It's not them. It's exactly what Molly told you; the show is too nasty; too mean-spirited."

Bob felt stumped. "I don't get it. Guys, it's just a show."

Molly nodded. "Yeah, see, that's the problem. To you it's just a show. But see, to us"—she made a gesture that included her seated boyfriend—"to us, it's too much like real life."

Ted explained: "Sure, man, Molly and I are one of those couples who bicker a lot, but deep down I really love her and she really loves me too."

"Yeah, even though we argue all the time, we know we don't really mean anything we're saying." She frowned. "But I don't understand how it works...but with everyone watching us up there...each time I say something...it's like I'm trying to find the thing which will hurt Ted the most. And afterwards, while the women in the audience are all cheering, I hate myself for doing so and I start questioning if I really, somewhere deep down in my soul, meant what I just said and—"

"It's called creativity," Bob said, not really believing what he was hearing but knowing that whether he believed it or not, his life and livelihood, and his sanity were at the moment on the line in a big way.

"Creativity my foot!" Ted spat and got up with anger etched all over his face. He stepped behind Molly's chair and after placing his hands on her shoulders, leaned over her, glaring at Bob. "Creativity be damned, man. I love this woman"— his declaration making the seemingly-near-tears Molly reach up and pat his hands—"and I hate saying all those hateful things about her. It makes me feel horrible afterwards and I hate that and...and then I remember what she's just said about me too and I want to say something even worse about her, and I begin wondering if she actually means the nasty things she said about me; I mean, if she's been harboring those thoughts in her mind all along." He fixed Bob with a piercing stare, one that made Bob want to shrink into a safe wrinkle in his chair's upholstery. "Man, each time we perform *Marriage and Divorce* I feel like I'm going crazy."

"And I feel like I need a shrink and antidepressants," Molly hotly declared.

"And so, we both want out of this insanity of yours. We quit."

"Yeah, any more of *Marriage and Divorce* and I'll never want to get married!"

"But you're on your way to being famous," Bob protested weakly. "Think of that. We're already getting lucrative offers from Broadway. One month from now you'll both be A-listers."

"I'd rather be unknown and happy with the woman I love," Ted declared with deep passion from behind Molly while massaging her shoulders, "than have all the money in the world and be as miserable as I am now."

"Hell yeah, me too!" Molly seconded him. "I mean, money's great for sure, and everyone needs it; but at the end of the day, it's all about who you share that money with, right? And if you ever gave me a choice between a pile of cash and Teddy"— she grinned up at him—"I know what my answer's gonna be. I'll take my Teddy bear any day."

"Sorry, dude," Ted said after bending to kiss the top of Molly's head, "we hate to put you on the spot like this, but this has gotta end right here and right now. Maybe you really should rehire those Miller guys again."

Bob sat staring speechlessly at them, the completeness of his horror having leeched his tongue of words. His mind however railed at the unsympathetic heavens: *Oh no, dear God, this can't just have happened to me again. It can't happen to me! Not right now when I've just gotten the biggest break of my life.*

He stared pleadingly at Ted and Molly. "Please guys, don't do this to me."

They both shook their heads. Ted took a step backward from Molly's chair and she got up too. Hand-in-hand they prepared to leave.

"Sorry, but for us it just ain't worth it, man," Ted said.

"Whoa, now hold on, you two. Just you hold on a minute," Lisa said, stepping into the office.

Bob had never been so pleased to see her in his life. "They just quit on me."

"I know," Lisa said. "I heard everything outside in the corridor." A cold and calculating look on her face, she gestured to Ted and Molly. "Sit your behinds back down in those chairs, you two, and let's talk business."

"Our minds are made up," Molly protested, but she and Ted sat back down nonetheless.

"Good." Lisa walked over to sit on Bob's desk. Smiling coolly at him, she draped her fingers over his. Bob made no attempt to detach his hand from hers. It felt really nice to have someone on his side that he could actually rely on.

"Okay, now," Lisa said, "let's reopen negotiations. For a start, let's discuss your salaries. What's Bobby paying you at the moment?"

"Standard union rates," Ted said.

Molly nodded. "We're not certain how much that is, but since it's standard, it has to be good, right? Teddy figured that the basic pay for actors has to be much better than that for waitresses and elevator repairmen. It's why we both quit our jobs to do this."

Lisa laughed. "Yeah, most definitely. Okay, how about if Bob and I offer you triple that amount? So, from now on you'll each be getting triple standard union rates."

"Triple?" Molly asked, turning to look first at her boyfriend then back at both of them. "You'll pay us three times as much?"

"You're serious?" Ted asked, his eyes reflecting his interest. Both he and Molly were clearly warring with their consciences, but Lisa's financial offer clearly seemed too good to them to turn down.

"We're dead serious," Bob agreed. He figured they were worth it. None of his replacement cast had been paid yet. The Barnaby's standard pay—at least what he'd been paying the Millers—was $1166 per week per actor. He definitely valued Ted and Molly at thrice that.

"Okay, that's good," Molly said. "That's fine with us."

"But how about the show's mean-spirited content?" Ted asked. "That's the main problem here. We don't like to be calling one another names on stage all night."

"I see no problem with that," Lisa said. "You're the ones calling the shots as far as what you discuss on stage. You don't *have* to fight with one another. The important thing is that what you talk about has to be the travails of marital life."

Molly seemed struck by lightning at this revelation. "Hey, why didn't we think of that?"

"Only because you're new to acting, darling," Lisa sweetly replied.

"Yeah, I think that'll work," Ted said smiling. "We can discuss politics and sports and things like that."

"And window-shopping and fashion and cute babies," Molly added.

The next ten or so minutes were spent drawing up a list of topics that Ted and Molly and the rest of the cast could safely discuss on stage without resorting to mudslinging. Then Ted and Molly departed downstairs to go join the others to discuss the changes with them, with Bob promising to be down himself in short while to direct them once he'd gotten through discussing a few things with Lisa.

When the office door shut behind the pair, Bob heaved a huge sigh of relief. "Crisis averted, thank God!"

"Yeah, that was close," Lisa agreed. She pointed to the cabinet in the corner. "Pour me a drink, Bobby. I need it after that discussion."

"Me too." Bob got up and hurried over to the cabinet and retrieved the bottle of whiskey and two glasses.

"I'm still worried though," he admitted to Lisa while handing her drink to her. "Do you think they'll still be able to pull it off without the arguments? You know that's what the audience are really buying into, that conflict between the sexes which Ted and Molly so perfectly portray. It's like they're having an open argument and inviting all their friends and enemies to weigh in with their opinions."

Lisa sipped some whiskey and then laughed loudly. "You've no need to worry yourself on that account, Bobby darling," she said. She sat in Bob's chair, leaned back and put up her feet on his desk. "Just you wait and see. Those two are like fire and gasoline. Yes, they love each other passionately, but it's the sort of passion that means they're going to fight no matter what. Ted and Molly aren't arguing because they're angry with each other; it's simply the way they both express themselves best in their relationship. I'll bet you a hundred bucks that tonight's 'no insults and nastiness' show is gonna be the most vehement and successful one so far."

"Okay, that's a relief," Bob said. "For a moment I was worried that the show would lose its spark."

"Don't worry your head about it, hon. Sparks are all those two have."

"Oh, you're cold, Lisa. You don't care a dime about them, do you?"

"Oh, I do care a lot about them. So long as they make us money, honey, I care a great deal about Ted and Molly. And so should you, Bobby. You've been broke for way too long and now you need a major attitude adjustment in lots of areas." Lisa winked at Bob and preened herself, striking a seductive pose with her fingers running through her hair that she knew would catch his attention and excite him. "Stick with me, hon, and I promise to help you upgrade your outlook on employee management, along with other areas of your life."

Laughing some more, she tossed her head back, poured the rest of her drink down her throat and shoved the glass at Bob. "Another one, Bobby. Make it a double this time."

Bob poured fresh drinks for both of them. He watched Lisa as she sipped her whiskey; yeah, there was something about her that he liked a whole lot. He was very impressed with how easily she'd convinced Ted and Molly to continue with the show.

Lisa lowered her glass and shut her eyes, very aware that Bob was watching her with approval. She was a patient woman and well experienced in matters of the heart; she knew that all she had to do was wait for Bob to get over his breakup with Jane and he'd be hers. She had no need to rush; their constant work proximity would naturally bring them together as lovers.

It was a nice feeling, to be on their way to the very top together.

Bob finished his whiskey. "Okay, I'd better get downstairs to direct—"

But then Lisa opened her eyes again and yelped in fright, "Bob! Behind you! The window!" Then she lost her balance and got upended out of the chair and wound up sprawled on the floor.

Alarmed by the fear in Lisa's eyes, Bob immediately spun around toward the window of his office.

". . . OR WILL GET YOU!" a huge white placard in the window proclaimed in bold red letters. The giant wooden sign was held up by two sets of hands and most of its upper portion was concealed by the wall above the window, clearly because the window-washer's platform that its holders stood on was raised too high.

This wrong positioning was rectified a few seconds later. The window-washer platform was lowered until Bob could clearly see both the placard's lettering and the faces of the man and woman at the window.

It was Case and Helen Miller out there, and their sign read: "GIVE US BACK OUR JOBS, YOU RAT OR WILL GET YOU!"

Bob read the sign through twice and shook his head. The Millers glared angrily at him. The office window was shut because the day was a little chilly, so Bob couldn't hear what they were saying. After gesturing to the Millers to hold on for a little while, Bob turned away from them and looked for Lisa. Lisa was still on the floor; she was holding her head and grimacing.

"Are you okay?" he asked concernedly.

"Yes, but I've got one hell of a headache."

"Okay, don't move. I'll be with you in a minute," Bob told her.

That settled, he returned his attention to his traitorous ex-employees. He walked over to the window, unlatched it and lifted the sash.

"Listen, man, we're sorry," Case Miller gushed. "We just wanted to—"

"If you're going to protest an action, at least get your protest right," Bob interrupted him.

"What you talkin' 'bout, man?" Case asked, with his wife looking equally confused.

"Your sign," Bob enlightened the pair. "There should be a comma after 'rat,' and it's 'we'll'...W...E...apostrophe...L...L...and not 'will'...W...I...L...L.' You spelt that wrong."

Case and Helen turned the sign around and examined it. "This is your doing," Helen told Case. "You should have let me write it."

"And concerning the question of my rehiring you guys," Bob said when the couple looked back up at him, "my answer is still 'No.' As you may have heard, I've currently got the best actors that ever lived working for me."

"Hey, dude, you can't do this to us!" Case sputtered.

"Yes, we worked with you for years!" Helen said.

Bob smiled. "Well, I do have some work for both of you."

He waited until they'd calmed down and were smiling hopefully at him before delivering the punchline: "Yes, I'll happily hire you guys to wash the theater's windows. At standard union rates, of course."

Then, while Case and Helen glared at him speechlessly in angry disbelief, Bob quickly closed the office window again, latched it shut, and while smiling broadly at the Millers, pulled the drapes shut too.

Then, ignoring the couple's muffled protests and knocks on the glass, and with a warm feeling in his belly which was only partly due to the alcohol he'd consumed, he crossed his office to help Lisa up from the floor.

"You handled that very well," she told him admiringly.

Bob grinned back. "Oh, I learnt it from you. Here, sit down in the chair and let me get you some aspirin."

CHAPTER 13

Oh, my dear God, what a horrible mistake I've made, Jane thought as she made her way up the theater stairs. *Bob was telling me the truth and I kicked him out!*

It had taken Jane Piper a whole week to get up the courage to come and apologize to Bob Barnaby. She'd quickly realized she'd overreacted. Talking to Molly on the night of the premiere of *Marriage and Divorce* had confirmed Fergie's story that Bob had hired his entire current cast outside of her apartment building.

She'd have apologized to him that night, but he'd been surrounded by pressmen and critics and there was no way she could have gotten him alone. So, she'd gone home, planning to say she was sorry the next day.

One thing she was really regretting now, was that she'd not simply sent him a text message that night. She'd wanted to see him in person. She felt it was the right thing to do after treating him so badly. And it would have been.

But then, to her surprise, had come the play's roaring success.

And that had changed everything. Previously unknown Bob Barnaby had become a superstar overnight, and now everyone wanted a piece of him.

And this had put poor Jane in a very uncomfortable position: if she apologized to Bob now and tried to get back together with him, she was going to look like a fair-weather girlfriend, someone who was only there for the good times.

Dammit, I should just have sent him that text that night. She felt like kicking herself.

"Hi, Jane!"

Jane realized she'd just reached the third-floor landing. Startled from her thoughts, she looked down the corridor and saw Dave Ferguson grinning at her. The old man was leaning on his mop, with the floor beyond him bearing testament to his cleaning prowess.

She walked towards him. "Hi, Fergie, how's things around here?"

The old man shrugged. "Not good. There's people everywhere all the time now, lots of muddy feet 'cos a the rains, so I gotta keep cleaning or the place is gonna look like a pig sty."

Jane nodded sympathetically, relieved to have these few moments to collect herself before she had to tackle the seemingly impossible task of convincing her ex that she wasn't just back to leech off him.

"Is Bob in his office?" she asked Fergie. "They're rehearsing without him downstairs and I wondered..." She hadn't dared call before coming over; she'd just taken a chance that he'd still be keeping his regular office hours, which would place him here at about now.

"Yeah, yeah, he is," Fergie confirmed. "I think Lisa's with him too."

"Lisa Manning?"

Fergie nodded. "Yeah, she's here all the time nowadays. Since the show took off, she and Bob have lots of business discussions together." Then Fergie gave Jane a searching look. "You know, it's odd. I'd have thought that now that Bob's successful again I'd be seeing you around here more often. A successful man needs his woman by his side. You know what I mean?"

Jane gulped and nodded. "I've just been really busy at work," she said. "They're thinking of promoting me and I—"

Fergie nodded. "Yeah, I get ya, but what's the point of trying for a promotion now? Once you guys are married, you're gonna have to stop working anyway. You ain't gonna have the time to be waitressing; Bob's gonna want you with him when he starts traveling everywhere." He glanced back down the corridor and lowered his voice to a conspiratorial level. "Honey, I'd advise you to be really careful: not just of Lisa, but of all the glitzy showgirls that keep hovering around Bob nowadays. If you don't mind me saying so, it ain't wise to leave your prime piece of cheese out where the mice can see it."

It took all of Jane's willpower not to burst into tears. *Oh, my God, what have I gone and done!*

"Okay, you run along now," Fergie told her, "while I get on with cleaning the floors. Though God know why I bother; give it an hour and they'll be all muddy again."

Jane nodded and walked off towards Bob's office. Lisa's presence there was an unexpected obstacle—Jane honestly couldn't be expected to grovel in front of her—but it wasn't an insurmountable one.

I'll just tell Bob I need to talk to him in private. He's hardly likely to refuse me with Lisa there.

But now that she was merely footsteps away from Bob's office, she slowed at the sound of Bob and Lisa's voices. The door to Bob's office was open and pair were laughing softly. Jane could smell alcohol, so the pair were presumably drinking as well.

Jane stopped by the door and listened.

"Wow, did you see their faces when I told them I'd hire them to wash the windows. They looked shell-shocked."

"Oh, it almost killed me not to laugh at them. But how naïve can one be? Did they really think you'd just sack Ted and Molly and rehire them instead?"

Jane figured they were talking about Case and Helen Miller, whom she'd seen driving off in their Dodge minivan when she'd arrived. The couple had been grim-faced, not acknowledging Jane's wave to them. Now she understood why.

"I think I will rehire them though," Bob said.

"Really?" Lisa sounded surprised. "But why would you do that?"

"I don't plan to sack Ted and Molly; that'd be suicidal for us. But I think I'll have Case and Helen work as their understudies. In addition to making them both eat humble pie, it's a great backup plan to avoid disaster if either of our stars suddenly becomes ill."

"Yeah, you're right. The way we've been doing it, we've been tempting fat.e In fact, we'd better rehire all the deserters, even the stage crew. Those two fat guys—sorry, I know it sounds unkind to call them that, but I can never remember their names...?"

"Ollie and Jerry."

"Yeah, the pair of them are seriously overworked."

"Yeah, sure. I agree with you. Okay, I'll let Case and Helen stew until the weekend and then rehire them."

Jane heard a clicking of glasses and then some sipping. And then Lisa said, "Alright, now that that's settled, there's something else we both need to discuss."

"Yeah? What's that?"

"Us. We need to discuss our own relationship."

Jane felt like she should rush into Bob's office right then and prevent Lisa from saying anything further. She could feel imminent disaster hovering over her, like an airplane about to crash from the sky onto her head. But at the same time she felt glued in place, and though her mind willed her to step through the door, and her heart began pumping blood through her arteries at an accelerated rate, she found herself paralyze by anticipation, totally unable to take a single step forward to save herself from her impending tragedy.

"Yeah," Bob agreed with Lisa. "I think so too. It's just that...well, I don't know why I'm still so hung up on Jane. It's like I can't get her out of my head. She treated me like garbage, threw me out of her house and yet, each time I think of her I still..."

"It's okay, darling," Lisa said. "I understand. A broken heart always takes a while to heal. The way Jane treated you was really nasty. I can't deny that I'm still shocked by it. I really thought she loved you."

I do! I do love him with all my heart! Jane thought.

But Bob laughed bitterly. "No, she didn't love me. All the greedy bitch wanted was a big wedding."

Jane wished she should unfreeze herself; but it wasn't happening. She tried her best, but her body just wouldn't cooperate with her mind. *No, baby, I don't want a big wedding anymore! I don't want to be famous in my hometown anymore! I just want to be with you forever and ever and ever! We can get married anywhere, with just two witnesses! I just want you back!*

"It's alright, darling," Lisa said. "I just want you to know that I'm here for you now. I'm all yours, Bobby, and I'm not hung up on wasting money like Jane was."

"Thanks," Bob said. "I'm glad I finally have a woman who understands me."

Jane now sensed the motion of bodies inside the office. She had the scary knowledge of what was about to happen. And then thankfully, she found that she could move again, she could take the five or six steps inside Bob's office and come face to face with the sight that she dreaded.

Bob was sitting on his desk with Lisa now standing in front of him. Bob was facing the far wall and so didn't see Jane enter, but Lisa did.

With the cold smile of a victor etched on her face, Lisa winked at Jane, and then, after quickly setting her drink down on Bob's desk, she took his head firmly in her hands and kissed him full on his lips.

Jane began weeping. Her eyes full of tears, she turned and fled Bob's office, running down the corridor and not even stopping when Fergie looked up from his mopping and called out to her, asking her what the matter was.

Oh, my God, I'm finished! I'm finished, was all she could think as she hurried down the stairs again.

CHAPTER 14

"Oops," Old Fergie said, leaning up on the handle of his mop again as Jane ran past him with tears streaming down her face. "I tried to warn the poor girl; but it looks like I was too late—the mice already got to the cheese she left out in the sun."

Then he sighed. "Damn, I just know this is gonna end badly."

CHAPTER 15

"And now, presented by the Barnaby Theater and Troupe featuring the best actors that ever lived, *Marriage and Divorce!*"

There was thunderous applause: the stage curtains parted, and the play began.

As Lisa had cannily predicted, tonight's show blew all the previous ones out of the water.

Ted and Molly were both incredible. Try as hard as they might, the young couple simply couldn't stop their emotions from getting the better of them.

One of the high points of the show was the discussion/argument they had about sex, marriage and money.

On the surface Lisa's suggestion had seemed innocent enough: "Just discuss how money or the lack of it—in short a couple's financial state—affects their relationship and the balance of power between the sexes in general."

And they'd started off genially enough:

"And so, by accident or design or general conspiracy," Molly said, "Men have more money than us poor women and we have to slave under them."

All the women in the audience loudly applauded.

"When you say 'under,' darling," Bob asked, "do you mean it figuratively or literally? I mean, does that include 'slaving under us' in bed too? Because if it does, I could do with you slaving a little now."

Molly growled at him. It was the men's turn to applaud.

And so, the banter went on. But then Ted, as was usual, put his foot in it:

"Why is it?" he asked the house in general, "that we never see a rich man with an ugly wife? I mean, the rich guys marry all the gorgeous women, and the rest of us are left with—?"

"What the hell?" Molly screamed before he could finish. "Are you saying I'm not pretty enough for you!?"

Ted realized he'd made a critical blunder. "No, no, honey, that's not what I mean. It's just that generally speaking, the richer a man is, the better looking his wife tends to be."

"There, you've just repeated yourself. What the hell do you mean I'm not pretty, you Elvis-without-a-Graceland?"

The entire theater audience burst into laugher.

"Yeah, yeah, yeah," Ted angrily agreed. "That's my whole point, girl. I don't have a Graceland of my own and so you're not Priscilla either."

Molly threw a prop cellphone at him.

"Hey, don't break it. That iPhone I got you for your birthday cost a huge chunk of my last paycheck!"

"Well, maybe if you were more of a man, your paycheck would be bigger and then," she began prancing about the stage, "and then I could afford plastic surgery just like other rich men's wives."

"Please, honey, I love you just the way you are."

She turned sweetly to face him. "Only you'd rather be richer?"

"Of course, I would. Who wouldn't?"

"Then you *don't* love me the way I am!" Molly shrilled. "You want a rich man's trophy wife." She turned away from Ted and strode towards the edge of the stage to address the women. "See, that's the thing, girls. We got no choice but to keep selling ourselves to the highest bidders. I've given that rat there"—a dismissive gesture over her shoulder—""the best years of my young life, and what's he do with it? He's already planning how he'll replace me once I'm over the hill!"

"Honey, I'm not planning to replace you."

Molly whirled on him and sank her fangs in. "Of course not, darling. You really can't *afford* my replacement yet. Pretty girls tend to be very high maintenance; not for your broke-ass kind of guy. You need to wait in line, wait patiently till you make it to the top, if you ever do. The sort of girl you want—the scheming little plastic surgery addict—probably spends more money on clothes in a month than you currently earn in a year."

The women all had a raucous laugh over that.

CHAPTER 16

After several nights of troubled sleep, ones that she spent tossing and turning on her large bed while constantly being tormented by nightmares of Lisa getting married to Bob in the 'Grandest Wedding of All Time' that was rightfully hers, Jane decided it was time to take positive action to end her romantic crisis.

If I don't do something today, I'll never forgive myself, she thought. *I have to let Bob know that I still love him, and that I'm really sorry that I hurt him so badly.* She sighed. *I really don't know how I can do that with Lisa now hanging around him; but at least I need to make the attempt. Then it's up to the fates.*

At first she thought she'd send him a lengthy message on Facebook; but then she'd discovered that he'd blocked. That hurt her a lot and she spent most of her morning at work wiping away tears.

It wasn't until closing time, when Jane was clocking out in the restaurant's staff room and staring at Molly's empty locker, that the solution to her problem hit her.

I'll simply ask Molly to intercede on my behalf!

Once this solution occurred to her, Jane wondered how she could have been so blind all this while. *As one of the stars of Bob's show, Molly most likely*

*has access to Bob whenever she wants to see him. Lisa won't
interfere if Molly says she needs to talk to the boss in private;
nor will Lisa suspect that their talk has anything to do with
me. Bob is certain to listen to Molly. Yes, he will! I heard
him tell Lisa that he still thinks about me!*

Jane instantly felt a lot more cheerful. *All I've got
to do is arrive at the theater a good while before the show
starts, so I can catch Molly in her dressing room.*

***

Ah, but the best laid plans really do go wrong.

A short nap to make up for last night's bad sleep
went on for too long and Jane arrived at the Barnaby
Theater at 8 p.m., an hour later than planned, by
which time the theater parking lot was already filled
with cars and a crowd of people queuing up at the
entrance and awaiting their turns to enter the
building.

8 p.m. was also just thirty minutes to showtime,
when Molly was sure to be busy making last minute
adjustments to her makeup and stage costume. But
Jane was desperate, and had the sense of the clock
ticking against her; every second she spent away
from Bob, every moment she delayed in letting him
know that she was sorry she'd hurt him, was
additional time for Lisa to flush her out of Bob's
affections and entrench herself in them instead.

Jane cursed her arriving so late. She was in too much of a hurry to join the lines of people climbing the steps and figured that if she tried to force her way through them, the newly employed security guard, whom she suspected was really just there to ensure that the Millers didn't enter the building, would quickly turn her away.

So instead, after checking her watch and realizing she had just twenty-three minutes left now before the show began, Jane hurried around the left side of the theater building to try the staff entrance at the back. She hoped it was open, because if it wasn't she was going to have to go back and join the long queues at the entrance, which meant that she might as well go home instead, as Molly was certain to have gone onstage before she'd be able to enter the building.

On her way there, she tried to work out how she was going to compress everything she had to tell Molly into a few concise sentences.

The most needful thing is to keep it short and sweet. I'll ask her to tell him that I need to speak to him; speak to him in private, somewhere where I'm sure Lisa won't be. Yes, that should do it.

Her gamble had paid off; the rear staff entrance was unlocked, and she quickly slipped inside and hurried along the dark back corridors towards the dressing rooms.

Molly's dressing room was on the left. Jane knew this from her visit here on premiere night. With a wave and a greeting, she hurried past the two overweight stagehands, who were moving pots of flowers in the same direction she was headed, and then she was in the corridor that led to the dressing rooms.

Only problem now was, Jane no longer remembered which dressing room was Molly's.

But here fate leant her a hand. With relief, she saw old Fergie enter the other end of the corridor. Fergie, apparently through for the day, was pushing a laden cleaning cart towards the cleaning closet between the second and third dressing rooms on the right.

Jane hurried towards the old man. "Oh, Fergie, am I glad to see you. Hey, which dressing room is Molly's?"

Fergie regarded her in surprise. "Jane? What're you doing down here?"

She scowled. "It'll take way too long to explain in any detail. Short version is, I'm trying to get my cheese back from the mouse that stole it."

Fergie laughed and pointed. "Great. Molly's is the third door on the left. But you'd better hurry, girl; you've just a quarter hour till showtime. The theater's almost full already and most of the cast are already backstage. Molly's still in her dressing room though. One of the other girls even asked me to see what's keeping her."

Jane pressed Fergie's arm in gratitude. "Thanks." Then she hurried off to the door he'd indicated and knocked. "Hey, Molly, it's Jane. Let me in, I gotta talk to you! It's really urgent."

At first there was no reply from behind the door, and Jane thought that maybe Fergie had been mistaken and that Molly was in fact upstairs with the other actors.

Just to make certain however, Jane rapped her knuckles harder on the door. "Hey, Molly, if you're in there, open the damn door. This is super urgent!"

This time the door did swing open.

"Yesh?" Molly asked. To Jane's surprise, Molly was still wearing her street clothes and hadn't yet put on her makeup. And in addition, she was swaying unsteadily on her feet, with a wine glass in her hand. "Tizat you Jane? Oh allrat, youse comminside...whats you want wimme anway?"

Jane couldn't reply. Molly was dead drunk. From the bottled evidence on her dresser table, she'd singlehandedly consumed at least two full bottles of wine, and had been two-thirds of the way through a third bottle when Jane had interrupted her.

Looking like she was going to slump to the floor at any moment, Molly shook her almost empty glass at Jane. "Heys, gurl, youse wants a drink?"

Jane was appalled. She glanced back down the corridor. But old Fergie had gone now and she was left alone with Molly.

Well at least I tried, Jane thought miserably, accepting that her purpose in coming here tonight was already defeated, because in Molly's current totally inebriated state there was clearly, absolutely, utterly no way at all that she was going to be able to understand what Jane had come here to ask her help with tonight, speak less of her later remembering to convey said message to its intended male target.

Feeling terrible about the way her plans had gone wrong, Jane stepped into Molly's dressing room and shut the door behind her.

Molly retreated to sit on her dressing table chair and reached for the almost-empty wine bottle. She tried pouring the wine into her glass, but her hands were too unsteady. Finally, she let the glass fall to the floor and put the mouth of the bottle to her lips and took a long, long pull.

Then she licked her lips and stared bleary-eyed at Jane. " 'Ello, gurlsie, s'whats you wants?"

"What's wrong with you?" Jane asked. "You're got a show to do in"—she glanced at her phone—"ten minutes."

"Cant'se do no damm shows no morz!" Molly exclaimed with wild gestures as if she was onstage. "All'se I evers doos iz cuss Teddy...telling him lies dat I'se hates...hates, hates, him whens I'se loves him with alla my hearts. No mores, no mores."

"Listen," Jane said, suddenly very very very worried for Bob's future if Molly didn't go on stage tonight as scheduled. "Yes, I know that acting can sometimes be hard, but you really need to sober up fast and..."

Molly put the bottle to her lips again. "Hells nope. Not gonna tells Teddy I hates him no mores...cos I truly luvvvvvs hims. I'm dones wizz this actress nons...nons...nonsenzzzzeeee. Wanna havs baybees! Lotsa pretty baybeeees!"

"C'mon, girl, you can't do this to Bob and me!" Jane tried to snatch the bottle away from Molly, but Molly ducked away from her grasp, tilted the bottle to her lips one last time and in a long-frenzied glugging, drained it empty.

"Oophs, its all gonezy," she told Jane and then collapsed to the floor, where she lay unmoving.

Jane stared down at her in horror. "Hey, get up!" she said, bending down over Molly and shaking her fiercely. But Molly was out cold. She burped and her breath was so alcohol-infused that Jane gagged and had to straighten up again and just gape at her.

"Oh, my God, no, you crazy girl, you can't do this to Bob. Are you trying to ruin him or what?"

Jane really felt like murdering Molly. But then a wiser, if much scarier, course of action occurred to her:

Alright, girl, here's where you finally become an actress.

At this realization Jane's stage fright rushed at her like an enraged bull, but she calmly deflected it aside. Her calmness surprised her. *This isn't something I want to do,* she thought as she quickly stripped off her clothes and pulled on Molly's stage dress. *This is something I NEED to do to help Bob out. I've no choice in the matter. As far as I can tell, this show doesn't have any understudies and all the other members of the cast have fixed roles. So if I don't go onstage in Molly's place, all of Bob's hard work up to this point just might end in ridicule.*

With this settled in her mind, Jane took a brunette wig off of a peg on the wall and slipped it on her head. Then she sat in front of the dresser and began applying makeup like she remembered Molly did.

CHAPTER 17

On the other side of the Barnaby Theater, where the men's dressing rooms were situated, Ted Miller was making his way towards the men's toilets.

The urge to ease himself had come over Ted all of a sudden. It wasn't a crisis moment and Ted wasn't hurrying along; he and Molly didn't go on stage till the third scene of the first act.

Hey, where is Molly anyway? What's keeping her?

The separation between the male and female dressing rooms meant that neither Ted nor any of the other actors gathered expectantly in the wings and waiting to go onstage had any idea about Molly's emotional meltdown.

Ted had a frown on his face; he looked like he'd eaten lemons for lunch. His current state of mind wasn't much better than his girlfriend's.

Okay, for sure Ted liked the fact that he and Molly were earning more money now (three times 'standard rates' had turned out to be quite a lot); and the fame and recognition were fantastic—"We're headed for the Big Apple, bay-be!"

But the price for these perks really didn't seem worth it. It was terrible going up on stage night after night and talking trash about the woman one loved. And meanwhile Molly would be shrilling back at him in rage, having, just like himself, forgotten that this was 'performance-talk' and not an actual lovers' quarrel they were having.

Yeah, dude, it's crazy. I wish we were just acting from a script like actors are supposed to do. But no, Bob says our genius is the way we keep coming up with all this spontaneous stuff.

Ted could hear the audience out there now, male and female voices murmuring in anticipation of tonight's performance. In his depression they sounded like a flock of birds of carrion—vultures or buzzards—waiting to feast on the bleeding remnants after he and Molly had ripped each other's guts out with words that they really didn't mean—couldn't ever mean about each other—but which nonetheless cut and hurt like knives.

Ted stepped into the toilet. *Man, I really wish I was back fixing elevators. I don't get it...Lisa gave us a list of safe topics we could discuss onstage without getting worked up...and yet we went up on stage and...bang!...What the heck was that about the other night...about me planning on ditching her for a trophy wife somewhere down the line. And it's scary, looked like she was dead serious too!*

Ted finished his bathroom business and washed his hands. Then he stood for a few seconds checking himself out in the mirror over the washstand.

Yeah, he really did look like a young Elvis, something all the theater journalists had begun picking up on now. He looked smooth in his blue work suit with the white shirt and red tie; really handsome.

But Ted's eyes were red too and had crow's feet from the sheer stress of going onstage every night.

Damn, I can't believe how bad I look. But that's the crazy thing. I feel this way now, but once I get up on the stage, it's like I become someone else and...damn, I just don't understand it!

Then, just like that, Ted broke down and began crying. He wept and wept and wept, while through the toilet doorway came the sound of the audience's laughter as the show began with Louie and Tess up on stage.

I don't know how much longer I can do this, Ted thought with tears streaming down his face. *One more week of this and I'll be ready for the funny farm. Either that or I'm gonna break up with Molly and then . . .*

More audience laughter pulled Ted back to the moment. He got out a handkerchief from his suit pocket and wiped his face dry, and then turned to leave the toilet; he and Molly would be due on stage very soon.

Yeah, yeah, but that'll have to be later. I'm gonna have a talk with Bob and Lisa about us using some pre-scripted stuff. That way we won't have to . . .

In his preoccupied state of mind, Ted wasn't watching where he was going. He stepped on a bar of soap that had fallen onto the floor from another washstand.

"Whaaaaattt!?" Ted yelped as his left foot slipped out from under him. He desperately tried to right himself, but it was a futile effort. Arms flailing like mad, he went skidding along the floor towards the toilet entrance, which he hit hard.

Ted hit one side of the doorway, then he bounced off of that one and hit the other upright, this second time with his head, and very hard at that.

"Aw shucks!" Ted groaned in pain. Then his eyes rolled back in his head and he slumped to the floor unconscious.

And, sprawled across the toilet entrance—half in and half out—was where Fergie found Ted a minute later.

Fergie pulled Ted out of the doorway and tried to revive him, but the young man was out cold. He was clearly still alive—he was breathing heavily—but considering what was at stake here, Fergie found this to be scant reassurance.

"Oh no, this is really gonna end badly," the old man said, shaking his head in horror. Then he hurried away to tell the others the bad news.

CHAPTER 18

Bob and Lisa were preparing to leave his office and head downstairs to the amphitheater when Fergie entered and gave them the bad news.

Bob gaped at Fergie. "Ted did what?"

"He knocked himself out silly."

Bob turned to Lisa who was equally shocked. "He did what?"

Fergie patiently repeated himself: "The kid slipped on a soap bar that fell off of a washstand in the men's toilets; he's half near brained himself. He's unconscious; won't be performing anything tonight."

Bob and Lisa stared at each other a bit more.

"Where is he now?" Lisa asked.

Fergie jerked a thumb out through the office door. "Ollie and Jerry carried him back to his dressing room." He frowned. "But you're gonna have to think of something really quick. The guys and girls backstage are about to start panicking. Joe's just gone onstage now to do his soliloquy, which is the next thing in the script, but they don't know what they should do after that since that's when Ted and Molly should go onstage."

Bob, seeing disaster staring him in the face, stared at Lisa. "Baby, my mind's a total blank. What do we do now?"

Lisa thought for a moment, then lifted a finger when an idea came to her. "First thing we need to do is buy ourselves some time." She fixed her gaze on Fergie. "Alright, Bob and I will head down to Ted's dressing room and see if we can perform a miracle and revive him."

"I just told ya," Fergie said. "That ain't gonna be happening any time soon; at the moment I'm prayin' the kid don't have a concussion."

"Don't you worry about that, Fergie," Lisa said with steel in her voice. "We don't need to panic yet. But we do need to buy ourselves some time. So, Fergie, you go and tell the guys that once Joe comes off the stage, Rhonda and Barry should go on next and do their skit; not the first one—the long one about apples and oranges."

"But that's the third scene in act two," Bob protested. "The audience are gonna be expecting Ted and Molly next."

"It's an ad-libbed show," Lisa countered. "Don't you worry 'bout it, everyone will just think we rearranged things. The main point is that that 'Apples or Oranges?' skit is a long one—I think it's about eight minutes long?" She nodded at Fergie. "You go tell them that while we figure out what we can do."

Fergie nodded and hurried off to deliver the news.

Once he'd left, Bob looked at Lisa. "Okay, what now?" He slapped his palm against his face. "Damn, I should have rehired Case and Helen. Then we wouldn't be in this position. Running a hit show without understudies was simple courting disaster."

"Oh, it isn't your fault, darling," Lisa said, grabbing up her purse from Bob's desk. "Listen, I'm not really sure what we can do, but even if you could rehire your band of deserters right away, there's no way they'd be here in the next ten minutes."

"Yeah," Bob glumly agreed. "So, what now?"

Lisa frowned. "So, we'll have to improvise." She tugged on his sleeve. "Come on, let's hurry down to Ted's dressing room."

They stepped out into the corridor and ran down the stairs.

***

Ted was lying on his back on the floor. Kneeling beside him was the stagehand Jerry.

Jerry looked up in relief when Bob and Lisa entered.

"What the hell are we gonna do now?" Jerry asked. "I've been trying to rouse him, but I can't." He gestured to a bottle of water on the floor beside him. "I've even tried the old 'water-in-the-face' technique, but he just won't wake up."

"Move over, let me have a look at him." Jerry shifted a bit and Lisa knelt down beside Ted. With calm and practical gestures, she examined Ted's pulse and peeled back his eyelids and examined his eyes, then she looked up at Bob and shook her head. "Forget about waking him up anytime soon."

Bob nodded but didn't speak. He was listening to the audience. The crowd's laughter was still going loud and strong. "No crisis as yet," he told Lisa. "But now what?"

"Take his clothes off," Lisa instructed Jerry.

He looked at her in surprise. "Why?"

She shrugged. "Because Bob's going to put them on."

Now it was Bob's turn to stare at Lisa in surprise. "What?"

She nodded sweetly at him. "Of course, darling. You and Ted are about the same height. Okay, you're a bit heavier than he is, but your voices have about the same timbre. And what's more, as the show's producer and director you know all the parts better than anyone else."

Bob stared at Jerry, who hadn't yet begun carrying out Lisa's instructions and who equally stared back at him. Then he looked down at Ted.

Ever since he and Lisa had left his office, Bob Barnaby had had the feeling that Lisa was going to suggest just this course of action, that he substitute for his fallen actor, take the stage in his place.

"I'm not sure this is a good idea at all," he said. "The audience will definitely notice the difference."

Lisa nodded. "Stop making excuses. Sure, they'll notice. We can count on that happening. But anyone who doesn't know you in person will think you're Ted's understudy."

"I'm not a good actor."

Lisa grabbed him by the shoulders and looked him squarely in the eye. "Who cares? Bob, you've got a degree in Theatre Arts studies. You've been running this damn theater for over a decade now. You can act. You can do it!"

Bob shook his head. "I just know this gonna end badly."

"That's old Fergie's line," Lisa pointed out and both she and Jerry began laughing. She gestured to Jerry again. "Take Ted's clothes off and hurry up with it; we've got a show to save."

She turned back to Bob. "Well, what're you waiting for, darling? Start getting undressed too."

Bob had forgotten that part. "Yeah, sure," he gulped and began stripping.

Yeah, but she's right, isn't she? he thought as he undressed. *It is my show and I'm really the only one who can save it now.*

CHAPTER 19

"Hey, who're you?" Louie asked when Jane stepped into the wings in Molly's place.

"I'm Molly's understudy," Jane replied. She knew that this was the really awkward part of her plan. This guy Louie really had no idea who she was.

"What's an understudy? Tess asked, stepping up to the pair. Then, after giving Jane a once-over, the energetic young blonde added: "And where's Molly?"

"Molly's drunk," Jane explained to Tess. Then she looked at Louie, who stared at her in bewilderment. "I'm here to take Molly's place on stage because she's in no position to perform tonight."

She peered out onto the stage. The audience were laughing loudly while Rhonda explained that women were 'oranges,' soft and yielding fruit that could easily be peeled to reach the juicy goodness within, but men were 'apples,' hard fruit which, although also delicious, needed to be violently bitten or sliced open to get any good out of them.

"Damn, it never rains, but it pours," Louie said, "First Ted and now Molly? Both in one night? What the hell else is gonna happen tonight?"

Jane had no idea what he was talking about. She shrugged at Tess who was scowling at her in suspicion and then pointed back towards the ladies' dressing rooms. "Hey, girl, I didn't attack Molly, if that's what you're thinking. If you don't believe my story, you can go see for yourself. In Molly's current state, she's giving the drunken skunk a bad name."

"Hey, man, keep an eye on her while I go see if she's telling the truth," Tess said and then hurried off to go confirm Jane's tale.

Louie nodded and then stared at Jane. "Yeah, so what's an understudy?"

Jane explained this most basic of theater principles to the man, but only half of her mind was on their conversation. Out on the stage, the 'Apples or Oranges?' skit was rolling on through its usual hilarious success, with the audience none the wiser as to why it had been moved forward tonight. Jane herself was aware that this scene should actually come up about midway in the play; but she didn't suspect anything was amiss, mainly because, now that she was so close to the stage she had begun feeling the usual stage fright butterflies fluttering in her belly.

But I need to do this, I do need to do this, she told herself fiercely. *Yes, I tend to freeze up onstage, but I won't tonight. Tonight, I'm going to break the jinx. I don't care how I do it, but I will do it. I have to help Bob out here; Bob needs me tonight and I can't let him down. Even if it kills me to go on the stage, I won't let Bob down.*

Tess arrived back from the ladies' dressing rooms then, along with Linda, the final female member of the play's small cast, and Fergie.

"She's telling the truth," Tess gasped in shock. "Molly single-handedly polished off three bottles of champagne. The only acting she's doing tonight is in dreamland." Then she looked curiously at Jane. "Hey, that name you called yourself again. Understudent or what was it?"

"Understudy?" Jane corrected her.

"Yeah, what's one of those?"

"Come here, hon, and let me explain," Louie told Tess and took her aside.

"Who are you anyway?" Linda asked Jane.

"Leave her be," Fergie said. "She's Bob's girlfriend."

Jane felt grateful to him for that. The statement gave her instant stature in the actors' eyes.

"But, hey, I thought, Bob was dating Lisa," Tess called out from aside.

"Not for long, he isn't," Jane muttered angrily under her breath. Now she really had huge motivation to get onstage and do her best. How dare Lisa usurp her rightful place at Bob's side? Her glorious wedding dreams flashed before her eyes and then transformed into her nightmares of Lisa being the one getting married in her place.

NEVER! Jane would NEVER permit that to happen. NEVER!

Out on the stage the applause from the audience was both thunderous and rapturous. The sound galvanized Jane. *Oh, tonight I'm gonna do a whole lot better than you guys. I'm a real actress, not some untrained amateur who Bob found out on the street!*

Jane felt so indignant that she hardly realized Jerry was clipping a wireless microphone to her collar. Nor did she realize at first that Fergie was talking to her; not until he tapped her on the shoulder.

"Oh..." She gave a start and turned to him. "Sorry, what were you saying?"

The old man leaned in close and whispered: "You're being very brave tonight. I know how scared you are of acting on stage. I'm just worried because Ted—"

Jane hadn't really been concerned on not seeing Ted tonight, because she knew he usually entered the stage from its opposite side. And old Fergie never got to tell Jane what had happened to Ted anyway, because right then Rhonda and Barry came off the stage to thunderous applause which drowned out his whispering, and Ollie stepped up to them and said. "Okay, time for the first living room scene—you're on, Molly!"

Jane winked at Fergie. "He means *me*, of course. Wish me luck."

Fergie made a 'fingers crossed' sign and Jane turned and rushed onto the stage.

CHAPTER 20

Fergie took one look at the opposite stage entrance, saw who it was that was coming onstage in Ted's place, and sighed so loudly that everyone around him turned to stare at him.

"What's the matter, sir?" Tess asked.

Fergie pointed to the stage. "I just got a feeling that this is all gonna end badly," he said.

They all turned and looked at the stage again.

"Hey, guys, is that *Bob* dressed up as Ted?" Louie asked in a confused voice.

Struck speechless by the totally unexpected sight, the others all just gaped.

"Oh yeah, this is definitely gonna end really badly," Fergie repeated.

Everyone nodded their agreement.

CHAPTER 21

Jane was the only person in the theater who at first didn't notice that Bob, and not Ted, was her partner on stage.

This was because the moment she set her feet on the smooth wooden planking, her stage fright wrapped her up like a blanket.

She managed to keep walking until she was near the chair in which Molly usually sat in this scene. But then, like water becoming an icicle, she froze up. She stood there on stage with noise in her ears and mind and the feeling that the sky was falling on her.

Oh no, not again! she thought in fright. *Not on tonight of all nights!*

But there was no helping it. She recalled the usual advice on how to combat stage fright that she'd been given during her acting classes: forget the stakes, concentrate on the performance, slow down.

"Breathe deeply, as if you're performing a vocal yoga exercise," was what Bob used to tell her.

Jane tried all of these now, but none worked. She still felt petrified, glued in place on that portion of stage with the spotlight hot on her and the audience expecting her to entertain them.

She managed to turn and look at the audience, all these spectators to her inevitable downfall.

And yes, it was inevitable that I was simply going to screw things up once I got on stage, and . . .

But then Jane realized that the audience were looking confused. Everyone kept looking from her to Ted and back again.

So finally, Jane too looked up at 'Ted.'

Her stage fright instantly vanished. She completely forgot that she was acting, with an audience of four hundred people watching her.

"Bob?" she gasped, her paralysis slipping away from her and enabling her to walk over to him and whisper from a close distance. "Bobby, what are you doing on stage?"

***

"I should ask you the same question," Bob said, being as startled to see her as she was to see him. "Hey, you didn't knock Molly out and take her place just to make me look bad, did you?"

"No, I didn't knock Molly out," Jane replied heatedly. "At the moment, your beloved best-actress-who-ever-lived star is drunker that fifteen winos combined, and I figured the least I could do was take her place on stage."

"I wonder why," Bob smirked at her. "I'd have thought you'd be delighted to see me in this big of a mess."

"And what are *you* doing in Ted's stage clothes anyway?" Jane asked angrily. "Or did you get jealous of all the acclaim he was getting instead of you and bump him off?"

"Of course not," Bob protested, leaning back indignantly. "Ted had a little accident in the bathroom."

Jane sniggered. "Which I'm sure you arranged, didn't you?"

"Of course, I didn't knock Ted out."

"Are you *sure* about that?" Jane asked. "The Millers were right to quit before you got envious of their talent and bumped them off too."

Bob was preparing to angrily retort to this, but then . . .

"Hey, are you two going to do anything else tonight beside bitch at each other like caged tigers?" a male voice called from the audience.

Jane stared at Bob in horror. "Can they hear us?" she whispered.

"Yes, of course we can all hear you," a woman in the audience loudly confirmed. "Your microphones are on."

Equally shocked, Bob stared at Jane. "But we were both whispering. Were our voices that loud?"

"They still are!" someone else shouted. "Get on with it, you two!"

Bob and Jane now both looked down at Lisa, who was seated right in front of them in the front row. Lisa looked horrified. She mouthed: "Yes, yes, you two idiots, your mics are capturing everything you're saying."

"Yeah, get on with it!" an old man seated up in the right wing of the gallery yelled down at them, leaning over the banister and shaking his fist at them. "So, we know now that Molly's drunk and Ted's had an accident and both of them can't perform tonight, but you two can! We spectators still wanna see a show, or don't we, folks!?"

"Yes, we do! Yes, we do!"

"Make it good one too!"

"Let's just give them a performance," Jane said. "We can fight afterwards."

"Yeah, alright," Bob agreed. "Just don't mess things up."

Jane's eyes flashed at him like fire. "If you dare say that one more time, Bob Barnaby, I'll...." she threatened him, heedless of who could hear them.

Then, while Bob waved and bowed apologetically to the audience, Jane turned and walked over to sit in her stage chair.

CHAPTER 22

Amongst other topics, this scene of the play dealt with loyalty and therefore Jane wasn't surprised when Bob accosted her with her own awful behavior toward him.

Bob: "Oh, darling. I've had an utterly horrible day at the office today, slaving away, and with the boss completely unappreciative of my efforts."

Jane: "I'm sorry to hear it, dear. Would you like a beer?"

Bob: "Yes, please. Oh, darling, you wouldn't believe what happened. "Case and Helen quit on us and the boss blames me, as the company's human relations manager, for letting them leave."

Jane (handing Bob his beer and looking annoyed because she didn't realize that while ad-libbing Bob had just used the first two names that came to his mind and wasn't actively targeting her): "But why would he do that, darling?"

Bob: I don't know, sweetheart. But the upshot of everything is that I now have to work double shifts; doing their jobs as well as mine. I'm sorry, honey, but our planned trip to Florida's gonna have to be cancelled."

Jane (seeing red and losing it): "Get out, you slimy rat! You're cancelling on me again? I hate you and I never ever, ever, in my life want to see you again."

***

The audience laughed. Bob, however, reliving the moment when Jane actually had kicked him out of her apartment and her life, immediately slipped out of character:

"You know," he said, walking up to Jane, "I honestly can't believe that the woman I loved with all of my heart could be so callous. I'd been working around the clock to build up this theater again, so you could have your lavish high-society wedding, and what did I get for it?"

Jane too now instantly reverted to her non-character self: "Hey, don't bring up the big wedding I wanted, this wasn't the fault of the damn wedding."

"Maybe not," Bob said heatedly. "But it most definitely played a major part in helping things deteriorate."

"How's that?" Jane asked dangerously.

"Well, sweetheart," Bob patiently explained, "if you'd not been so insistent on us getting married with all the A-listers on Broadway present, we'd be married by now."

The audience had now fallen completely silent and were listening to Bob and Jane with rapt attention. They still weren't certain what was going on, but they were certain of one thing: that what they were currently witnessing transcended mere acting; it had the 'truth' of an actual slice of life to it.

The only member of the audience who realized that Bob and Jane weren't acting anymore was Lisa, who, the longer this went on, got more and more of a sinking feeling in the pit of her stomach.

I don't even need to have Fergie here to tell me this is gonna end badly, Lisa thought.

"Bob, this is the *second* time that you've cancelled on me," Jane accused him. "The first time was last year after *Airplane Story* flopped. How do you think I felt?"

"Oh, Jane, please. Your mom warned you not to tell the entire village you were getting married.

"Clarksburg is not a village."

"It's just farms and horses and a trailer park. You guys don't even have a decent mall."

"I was born and raised there. The fact that it's small doesn't mean you can trivialize it."

"Yeah, whatever. But even putting that aside, this year I didn't put off the wedding. And I didn't break up with you either. All I did was tell you that the Millers quit on me the day before the show." He looked angrily at her. "And at that point in my life, when I was at my lowest, you kicked me out."

Then, as if inspired by the extent of his anger, Bob turned to the audience and pointed at Jane. "Yes, folks, when I was down and out, this woman here kicked me out. She said, 'Hit the road, Jack,' just like Ray Charles singing."

"Women do that to you all the time!" A man loudly proclaimed. "You have a little bad luck and they're like, 'Out the door, Chuck!' "

"Yeah, they do that!"

"Hey, not all women behave like that," a middle-aged woman protested. "I've been married for twenty-five years, and I'm still with Danny here."

"She really wishes she could kick me out!" Danny retorted. "But she's a double amputee with no feet!"

Everyone laughed.

"Hey, people," Jane said, stepping up to the edge of the stage, "Okay, so I was wrong there. I shouldn't have broken up with Bob like that. But...but how was I supposed to know that Bob was telling me the truth?" She looked around challengingly at the women. "Okay, girls, it's show-of-hands time. How many of you ladies in the audience haven't had a man try to wiggle his way out of marrying you by telling you some made-up story or the other?"

The only person to lift her hand was a young red-haired woman somewhere in the middle rows.

"Hey, miss!" Jane called out. "How many boyfriends have you had to date?"

"None," the redheaded girl admitted. "I really, really do want a boyfriend, but I'm scared to date anyone." She paused, then added, "Because, see, I've two older sisters who've both had boyfriends disappoint them when it came to time to get hitched. In fact, my sister Mary is crazy now because of this. That's the main reason why I don't have a boyfriend: I don't want to get dumped and go crazy too."

Jane turned and strode triumphantly back to face Bob. "This proves my point. Lying is the time-tested and typical male way of avoiding marital commitment."

"Hey, but I *wasn't* lying!" Bob protested.

"You *acted* like you were," Jane came back smoothly. "And, okay put that aside for just a moment. What did you do the moment I was out of the picture?"

Bob looked perplexed. "What *did* I do? What are you talking about?"

Jane walked back to the edge of the stage and pointed down at Lisa. "*She* is what I'm talking about.

The moment I turn my back on you, you start kissing that woman there."

"Hey, no I didn't," Bob protested.

"I saw you, Bob," Jane said. "Don't lie to me. I *saw* you kissing her. I came to your office to say I was sorry and there the two of you were, getting drunk and slobbering over each other."

Bob looked surprised. "You were in my office? When?"

"Three days ago. You don't have to take my word for it—ask Lisa, she saw me enter your office."

Bob turned to look at Lisa. "Honey, is this true?"

"Hey, don't ask me!" Lisa protested, throwing up her hands. "I don't want anything to do with this performance!"

The audience burst into laughter again. "More, more!" someone screamed from the gallery. "This is great stuff!"

"See, she admits it," Jane finished. "So, don't try to show me how righteous you are. Like most men, you were delighted to have me out of the way, so you could move on to your next conquest."

"Tell it like it is, girl!" a woman yelled from one of the middle rows of seats. Several of the women in the front three rows had begun eying Lisa angrily and gripping their handbags like they intended to give her a beating with them, and poor Lisa now cringed in her seat like an outed criminal. Lisa looked like she'd leap up at any moment now and run for one of the exits.

Bob waved at the angry women. "Hey, hey, ladies, leave Lisa alone. You're forgetting that she didn't engineer my breakup with Jane. She just moved into the house after"—he flung Jane an angry look—"after the so-called rightful owner of the residence left it. Jane kicked me to the curb and Lisa nicely gave me a ride in her car."

The women nodded and backed off. Lisa relaxed again.

"So, what are you gonna do about it, Bobby!?" a woman up in the left wing of the gallery asked.

"I really don't know," Bobby replied. "What do you think I should do?" Then spreading his arms in an all-encompassing gesture, he asked everyone in the house: "What do you guys think we—I mean Jane and I—should do?"

There was silence for few seconds and then the red-haired girl who'd never had a boyfriend before shouted, "You two should get back together! Kiss and make up!"

And then everyone in the audience began shouting it too. "Kiss and make up! Forgive and forget! Kiss and make up! Kiss and make up!"

CHAPTER 23

Bob heard the loud voices telling him what to do. But still, he felt conflicted.

Yes, Bob felt really conflicted over Lisa. Because, for selfish reasons or not, Lisa had stood by him loyally all this while. If she hadn't, Bob had no idea what he'd have done. And so, publicly dumping Lisa in front of everyone here tonight was the furthest thing from his mind.

He looked at Jane. Jane had tears in her eyes. "I'm sorry I treated you like I did," she wept loudly.

Staring at Jane crying like this, Bob felt as if his own heart was breaking too. It really didn't matter how she'd treated him anymore—it had never really mattered. He'd always be in love with Jane, no matter what. He felt like crying himself.

"Kiss and make up! Kiss and make up!" everyone yelled.

Bob looked down at the front row, at Lisa. Lisa had tears in her eyes too, but when he caught her eye, she smiled at him and nodded and pointed to Jane.

"Yes, take her back," she mouthed silently at him. "It's alright. I'm okay with it."

That was all the encouragement that Bob needed. "Yes, I forgive you, darling!" he told Jane and stretched his arms towards her.

Jane ran into his arms and hugged him. "Oh, I'm so sorry, so sorry, darling. I'll even forego the lavish wedding."

"No, don't forego the wedding!" the redhead shouted. "I'll set up a GoFundMe for you two to get married in the Bahamas!"

"Yes, yes, yes, yes, yes, yes, yes!" the audience screamed. "GoFundMe! GoFundMe!"

When Bob and Jane kissed the applause was so loud that the roof almost came off the building.

Finally, holding Jane tight, Bob turned to face the audience again.

"I want to say thank you to everyone here tonight for helping us get back together!"

"You're welcome!" a woman screamed. "Just don't break up again!"

Jane laughed. "Oh, I definitely promise not to kick him out again."

"And now, folks," Bob said laughing, "we're gonna try to finish the show."

CHAPTER 24

The next days reviews were unanimous: This truly was the best show ever; and the crew at the Barnaby Theater were truly 'the best actors that ever lived.'

"Hey, listen to what Harold Harrison wrote," Lisa told Bob the next morning in his office, then she read out loud from her phone: " 'Last night was surreal. It was one of those moments which a soul lives for, the sort of experience which, once witnessed, make one feel that one's life hasn't been lived in vain. Young Bob Barnaby proved beyond a shadow of a doubt that he was a master showman, and the memories from last night's show are some that I will fondly take to my grave with me. And once more, I defy any critics who disagree with me and repeat what I've said before—that last night, the best actors that ever lived really did occupy the Barnaby Theater's stage.' "

"That's pretty good," Bob said. "I just hope the old guy didn't get pulled over by the cops for drunk driving again."

"Here's another one, this from one of the feminist reviewers," Lisa said, tapping the screen of her phone. " 'Oh, what a great night, when the female spirit once more triumphed over the chauvinistic male patriarchy desperate to dominate it. Jane Piper demonstrated that if a woman has the willpower, she can accomplish anything she desires...including having the sort of wedding she wants.' "

Lisa looked up from her reading and laughed. "Boy, that was quite a show that you two put on last night."

Bob nodded and looked thoughtful. "Yeah, I know. But, Lisa, are you sure that you're okay with me and Jane getting back together the way we did? I mean it was very public and lots of folks knew that we were dating."

Lisa nodded. "Oh, yes, I'm very okay with it." She got up from her chair and sat on the edge of Bob's desk facing him and looked deep into his eyes. Then she laughed again. "You're too young for me anyway."

Bob laughed too.

"Where's Jane?" Lisa asked. "Wasn't she supposed to be here this morning?"

"She went to hand in her notice at work. She's due here any min—"

Then there was a loud tapping on his office window and Lisa, who was just turning that way, shrieked again.

Thankfully this time Lisa kept her balance and didn't topple off of Bob's desk. Bob stared past her, at his office's window. Once more, a huge white placard with red lettering filled the glass expanse and blocked off any view of the outside world.

'WHERE SORRY. PLEASE REHIGHER US!!!' it read.

It took Bob a moment to work out what the sign was actually supposed to read. Then he laughed. "I guess Helen Miller is as bad at spelling as her husband," he said and walked over to open the window.

As expected, it was the Millers out there again, once more standing on a window washer's platform.

"Okay, you're rehired," Bob told the couple. "Tell everyone they can have their jobs back."

"Everyone?" Case Miller asked in surprise. "But what about these new guys you've been using in our place?"

"Yeah, what's gonna happen to them?" Helen added, shifting about uneasily on the window washer's platform and hugging herself because of the chill in the morning air. "You gonna fire them all?"

Lisa walked over to the window to join the three of them. "No need to fire anyone. Ted and Molly have had about as much of stage performance as they care to," she said. "Ted says he'll be fine with a management position here in the theater—we'll need someone to handle things while Bob and Jane are traveling with the show, while Molly...Molly's just found out that she's pregnant—which was the real reason she drank herself into a stupor last night. She just wants to get married and have her baby."

Case and Helen both nodded.

"The others can be your understudies," Bob added. "You original guys can alternate the roles with them. Which brings me to one more thing: "Because of the show's success in its current version, we'll be altering the original script of *Marriage and Divorce* to incorporate some of Ted and Molly's and the others' ad-libs—they'll all get royalties for that too." He sighed. "Last night on stage I got a taste of what Ted and Molly meant when they said ad-libbing like that was emotionally crushing...and damn, was it heavy—you wind up saying stuff that you don't mean at all. Anyway, we'll be taking a lot of the sting and unpleasantness out of the script."

He looked at the Millers who nodded their understanding.

"Sure, that's fine with us," Helen agreed. Then she shivered. "Hey, guys, it's real cold out here. Can we come inside now?"

Bob nodded and peered down at the parking; then he stepped away from the window. "Yeah, sure, just don't fall as you're climbing in through the window, you two. I can't start shopping around again for a fresh pair of leads."

CHAPTER 25

Old Dave Ferguson was feeling happy as he mopped the Barnaby Theater's third floor. As he worked his way along the corridor, Fergie whistled a happy tune to himself and occasionally even danced left and right, the unfamiliar dance steps making his old joints creak. As he whistled, Fergie almost felt he could hear the corridor walls whistling in delighted chorus with him.

According to what Fergie had just heard downstairs from Case Miller, Bob Barnaby had now completely paid off his debt to the bank and the theater was fully his property again.

Fergie smiled. Yeah, things had righted themselves; he could once more work in a peaceful frame of mind, not worrying if he'd still have a job here tomorrow.

He was still smiling when he reached Bob's office. The door was open and peering inside, Fergie saw Bob and Jane holding one another and kissing.

Fergie stood there for a moment, leaning on the handle of his mop. Then he said, "Yeah, I've got a feeling that this is gonna end—"

After regaining her composure after being startled, Jane instantly pulled away from Bob and regarded Fergie with a stern smile. "Don't even think of saying that, Dave Ferguson."

Fergie laughed. "Ah, I'm just kiddin' you two lovebirds. What I was really gonna say is—Yeah, I got a feeling that this is gonna end just great!"

The three of them burst out laughing.

"Oh, yes, it certainly is," Jane agreed and kissed Bob again.

The End.